FALLEN PETALS
THE DECEPTION
THE DECEIT
& THE DAMNED

A
Tiffany Simonè
Novel

Tiffany Simoné
New York, New York

Edited By: Constance Diggs and Jessica Guzman
Cover Design By: Michael Drake 360 MEDIA
Photography By: Nile N. Johnson
Cover Model: Deleesa Carrasquillo

Graffiti Mural Design By: Various Street Artists
Harlem community activist Ray "Sting Ray" Rodriguez created *The Graffiti Hall of Fame* back in 1980 to provide a place for the city's talented graffiti artists to show off their skills. It's in the courtyard of the Jackie Robinson Educational Complex at 106 & Park Ave.

ISBN 13:978-0990613107
ISBN 10:0990613100

Printed in the United States of America

THIS BOOK IS DEDICATED TO MY SON

Ronnie Love

Thank you for bringing to my attention, what I could not see, my dreams deferred and my life at a standstill. I have been focusing on everything and everybody, except the talents that I have been given, to entertain through writing. I know I have what it takes but fear and rejection stopped me from moving forward. A lesson learned son, never put your dreams on hold, live life to the fullest, be fearless, and always remember:

"The Lord is my light and my salvation; who shall I fear? The Lord is the strength of my life; of whom shall I be afraid?" **PSALMS 27:1**

& TO MY SISTA, KAREN BROWN

You have been out of site, but never out of mind. I wish you were here today to share this moment with your friend. I need you to get-up from that bed and walk again. I need you to wake-up from that dark place that holds you hostage. I know you can do it. I've seen your strength, a single mother that raised three boys alone. I am here waiting for you, to laugh, and to cry, to be friends, and do what BFFs do, hang out and have a good time. I miss your carefree spirit, your smile, and your honesty. I miss you having my back, the words of encouragement when I need it most, and picking up the phone just to say, *"What you doing crazy lady?"*

God, it's been too long since Karen has been sick and shut-in, spend your angels with haste and bless us with a miracle today. AMEN.

"Greater love hath no man than this that a man lay down his life for his friends." - **JOHN 15:13**

ACKNOWLEDGMENTS

My attempt at writing my first novel has been a challenge. I didn't't think I could do it. I written a screenplay, but never a novel and didn't't know where to start. I had a lengthy conversation with my Uncle Michael (1st writer of the family), who said, "If you can write a screenplay, than you can write a novel". I sat at my computer, shut myself off from the world, very determined to write this novel and finished writing it, in a little over a month, thank you, Michael George for being my biggest motivator.

To friend, Robert Miles, what a surprise and blessing to receive your call and help, when I felt like my back was up against the wall and I didn't know how I was going to pull this off. I cannot thank you enough nor express with words how grateful I truly am. For sharing my dreams, for your invaluable support, I say thank you.

To my editors, Constance Diggs and Jessica Guzman, I can't thank you enough. It's been a long road of rewrites and never-ending edits, but we did it and my first book is final complete and ready to be self-published.

To Veronica Keitt and Michael Drake (360 Media), I appreciate you so much, the endless hours, your exceptional talents, and for putting up with my stickler for perfection. I know that if I continue to surround myself with people that work as hard as me, have the same goals, and dedication anything is possible. I do believe there is a bigger picture then this, I have my eye on the prize and you both can surely be apart of it. *P.S. Tell your niece Princess Smith, she may have been too young to shoot the cover, but she won't be too young to have a role in my first big movie.*

Deleesa Carrasquillo (Cover Model) and Nile N. Johnson (Photographer), two young people who give a new meaning to being true to your art and set the bar high when it comes to professionalism. All the obstacles you had to confront, getting up early on a Saturday morning, working in the rain, the long hours in the cold, etc. thank you for your patience, understanding, and giving me a novel cover that is not only a piece art, but the kind of perfection, I look for in everything I do.

Denisha Johnson-Williams, Meckha Cherry, Cleveland Manley, and The West 118th Street Cultural Association (WOSCA) for your invaluable help and support in everything I do, I say thank you.

Adriane Mack, Cory Brodnax (OSO Gemstone), Evetta Petty (Harlem's Heaven Hat Boutique), John Whyte, Leandra & Malique Sampson (Johnny Kaks International) Joseph Riley-Land (Riley-Land A Gourmet Pantry) and), Keith Longmore, Melanie & Bernardo Nieves (Avon), Michael Neal (Lot Keeper) you are not just my vendors at SoHA Square Open-Air Market, some of you have become very good friends, people that I can rely, and that provided me with your invaluable expertise.

Renee Moses (Hair Stylist) and Sade (Sade Skin Care), two people that always give you high-quality work. Every time I sit in your chair my hair and makeup is always flawless. Thank you for the perfect cover head shot.

I want to give a special shout-out to founder of Hue-Man Bookstore and Cafe in Harlem, Clara Villarosa for taking the time to stop and talk with a stranger. Your advice was valuable and your insights in the art of writing were immensely helpful.

To all my mom, grandma, family, true friends, and business associates, for being there in the mid-night hour with a listening ear, being honest and keeping it one-hundred, for your constant unconditional love, your acts of kindness, and support in my many ventures, thank you. And, special shouts to: Albert "Chubby" Crumes, Anthony Curry, Bobby Gregory, Chip Singh (Graphic Artist), Christal Cherry, Clarence "Gums" Williams, Debra

Garland (Cousin), Derrick "Vito" Jones, Denisha Williams, Eric Von Zip (R.I.P), Garnett Robotham (The Jackie Robinson Education Complex), Glendon Chancey III (Author of "The Coin"), Got Tested Crew, Gotham Writers Workshop Professors and Students, Jerry "Jameek" Mitchell, Janet and Jeanie Williams, Jerry Washington, Joseph "Li'l Joe" McLloyd, Karen Ramsey, Michelle Baptiste, Ms. Dee Dee Ford, Ms. Francis, Ms. Joyce Conoly-Simmons (CCNY mentor), Ms. Victoria, Oliver W. Martin III (R.I.P), Omar Ahmad, Richard Billingsley, Ronald P. Love (My Son's Father), Silvia Velez, Steve "CAS" Vializ (Graphic Artist), SoHA Square Market Vendors, the Moses Family, the Harp family, Todd Jones (Cuzin's Duzin), and Victor L. Cummings.

Again, thank you Robin Devonish-Scott (Consultant) so much for your help. I greatly appreciate the assistance you have provided me in self-publishing.

FALLEN PETALS
THE DECEPTION
THE DECEIT
& THE DAMNED

Be not deceived; God is not mocked: for whatsoever a man soweth, that shall he also reap. For he that soweth to his flesh shall of the flesh reap corruption; but he that soweth to the Spirit shall of the Spirit reap life everlasting. **GALATIANS 6:7-8**

1988

"He was my hero, until he showed me his true colors. The fantasy world my parents painted for me, as a child was a lie. I would find out through an unforeseen incident that this dream world did not exist. The people closest to you could not always be trusted. The truth did not always set you free. And, the real world was evil, dark, and defile, a nightmare I could not escape, that would change my life and set me on a path of self-destruction."

-Symoné Harris

BEGINNING OF THE END

· ·

CHAPTER 1

August 13, 1988

A sheltered, naïve, and preppy 17 year old, Symoné Harris, lives in the suburbs and has the perfect life.

Her boyfriend, Mike Blackwell, is New York City's most sought after high school basketball superstar. Her father, Vaughn, is a highly decorated police officer, and her mother, Mae, is listed as one of Harlem Hospital's honorary nurses.

Without a care in the world, Symoné admires herself while she stares in the mirror. She is wearing a pleated plaid skirt, oxford shirt, with a cardigan sweater loosely tied around the neck, and her hair is up in a neat bun with a big ribbon. She reaches in her jewelry box and puts on some pearls for her finishing touch.

Chrissy, Symone's best friend is stretched out on the bed turning pages of a magazine, as she bounces her head to the music video playing on the TV show Yo! MTV Raps. She's wearing fitted stonewashed jeans, with a matching tie-up shirt and a pair of blue high top Reebok. Her accessories include large gold bamboo earrings, a diamond nameplate necklace, with a matching bracelet, and a gold two-finger name ring. She is an around-the-way-girl from Harlem – tough and brutally honest.

"So what you think about my outfit, Chrissy?" Symoné asks.

She looks at Symoné and frowns. "Where you going dressed like Blair Warner from The Facts of Life?" Chrissy responds and then smiles.

Symoné scowls.

Chrissy continues, "We're going to the Rucker, Mike's championship game. You gotta look bangin'. Everybody's going to be there."

Frustrated, Chrissy tosses her copy of Essence aside, gets up off the bed, and walks over to Symoné's closet. She begins to rummage through the many clothes neatly arranged on hangers, throwing disapproved garments on the floor. She pulls out several jeans and tosses them to Symoné to try on. Once she approves of the fitted Jordache Jeans, she hands Symoné a pair of pink high top Reeboks. Chrissy then finds a matching shirt. She holds it up and yells, "Quick, gimme a scissor."

Symoné grabs a pair of scissors off her dresser and runs over and hands them to her. Chrissy quickly cuts the shirt into a replica of Jennifer Beals's gray ripped t-shirt in Flashdance.

Symoné looks on in disbelief. "My mother's going to kill me."

"Girl, it's just a t-shirt."

"An expensive one – which my mother brought."

"Here put this on." Chrissy hands her the shirt. "Now, sit down, so I can fix that hair before we miss the game." She starts flipping through the TV channels and stops on Channel 7 to the Eyewitness News Special Report on Tawana Brawley.

Symoné sits in front of the TV, while Chrissy plays with her long, shiny hair. Their eyes are glued to the screen. They are well aware of this story. There has been a media frenzy about it for weeks now.

"*Now, the Eyewitness News: Tawana Brawley was not the victim of a forcible sexual assault by multiply assailants over a four-day period. There is no evidence that a sexual assault even occurred . . . 15-year-old Tawana had been missing for four days when she was found in a trash bag, covered in feces with racial slurs written on her body. After being interviewed by police, Tawana indicated that she had been raped repeatedly by three white men, one of which was alleged a cop. During trial it was determined there was lack of evidence that she had been raped, and Tawana was even accused of creating the appearance of an attack herself . . .*"

Symoné is completely taken aback by what she's just heard. She shakes her head. "What? Wow, that's crazy. All that protesting, marching, lives destroyed, and for what?"

Chrissy roughly grabs Symoné by her hair to keep her still and get her attention.

"Ouch!"

"Don't be so quick to judge, something must've happened. Why would she put herself out there like that?" Chrissy argues.

"Only Tawana Brawley and the Lord know."

Symoné thinks nothing else of it and changes the channel. Chrissy lightly taps her hand with the comb.

❋ ❋ ❋

The sun is out and the Rucker's basketball park on 155th Street and Eighth Avenue is jam-packed. The championship game is tied, and there are still a few seconds left on the clock. Georgie, Mike's best friend steals the ball from the other side and dribbles it down the court with their star player, Mike, not too far behind. Georgie reaches the basket, throws the ball off the backboard, and Mike slams it down into the hoop with a windmill dunk. The crowd goes wild. Mike and Georgie's teammates hurry onto the court to congratulate them for a spectacular win.

The sunny clear blue sky has turned dark grey, and cloudy. It starts to drizzle.

"Mike, it looks like it's about to pour. Let's get outta here before we get caught," Georgie says.

"We out ya," Mike says to his teammates and hurries out the park with Georgie.

Suddenly the sky opens up and a heavy rain pours down. People are running out of the park to their cars or the train station across the street, and some take cover under the awnings at the nearby bodegas.

Symoné and Chrissy, are sitting in a jeep in front of the park.

"I'm glad we got back to the jeep before the rain," Chrissy says.

"Thank God. All the time it took me to find this outfit, and then have it ruin," Symoné responds.

"So, what's up? Going to the end-of-the-summer Hip Hop party at Sweet Cherry tonight?" Chrissy asks.

"Ain't that a strip club?" Symoné responds.

"Not tonight. Some Hip Hop promoter rented it out for a showcase and private party."

"How are we going to get past the bouncers? You know we don't even look twenty-one."

"My baby, Eddie knows the guys at the door. We'll go with him."

"I don't know why I asked. Mike's brother Eddie gets V.I.P. access into all the hottest parties. But, there's no way my father is gonna let me go to some hip hop party, and definitely not at Sweet Cherry."

"Spend the night at my house, and we'll leave for the party from there. Your parents don't have to know about the party."

"I don't like lying to my parents."

"You're not. You're spending the night at my house."

"Okay," Symoné reluctantly answers.

The driver-side door opens and Mike jumps into the seat, with Georgie climbing in the back with Chrissy. Mike kisses Symoné on the cheek and quickly takes off his wet basketball jersey. Symoné grabs a dry t-shirt off the armrest and hands it to him to put on.

"Good game, Mike," Symoné says.

"What? Did you expect less?" Mike says jokingly, then leans over and gives Symoné another kiss.

"Mike, you and Georgie are such showoffs," Chrissy exclaims.

"We were just giving the crowd what they came for," Mike responds with a smile.

"No doubt," Georgie interjects, and then he and Mike high-five.

"Where's Eddie?" Chrissy asks Mike.

"He had some business to take care of, but said that he'd see you tonight," Mike answers and then drives off.

❋ ❋ ❋

Sweet Cherry is crowded, the music is pumping, the dance floor is full, and everyone is dressed to impress. In Sweets's office at the back of the club, Detective Jack Fisher sits behind Sweets's desk, getting a blowjob from one of the strippers. He is an average sized man, somewhat over-weight, with a little beer-belly, a receding hairline, goatee, and a nervous habit of chewing on the inside of his bottom lip. She is an attractive young woman in a fitted, black cat suit and patent leather boots. Fisher is in ecstasy, leaning back with his eyes closed and holding the young woman's head down with both hands, as she reluctantly pleasures him. Sweets walks into his office. He is surprised to find Fisher. "What the fuck, man?"

The young woman is startled and appears relieved to have been caught. She hurries to her feet, wipes her mouth, and touches up her hair. She cuts her eyes at Fishers as she walks toward the door. Sweets takes a deep breath, gives the young woman a reassuring smile, puts a c-note in her hand, and she leaves the office.

"Damn Fisher, why you always messing with my girls? Time costs, man."

"Whatever, Sweets." Fisher says. He gets up from Sweets's chair, zips up his pants, and sits on Sweets's desk.

"I swear a woman is gonna be the death of you."

"You got my money, Sweets?" Fisher asks, and then picks up a shot glass and helps himself to the liquor on the desk.

"Yeah, I got it," Sweets replies. He then walks over to the safe and opens it. He takes out an envelope, puts it on the desk, and sits.

"So, did you get any information about the numbers Craig Little's pulling in?" Fisher asks.

"Little's killin' them, getting paid. He has a stash house in the Dunbar," Sweets confirms.

"Yeah," Fisher says, nodding in approval.

"That's the word on the streets," Sweets says, and then focuses his attention on the club's TV monitors on his desk.

Fisher pours himself another shot, and then walks over to the two-way mirror built into office wall, which overlooks the entire club floor. He scans the club, sees a familiar face in the crowd, and then frowns.

"I'm out, Sweets." Fisher takes an envelope off the desk, puts it into his pockets, and leaves.

❊ ❊ ❊

The young woman in the black cat suit is a bartender, serving drinks with another woman, who's wearing a tight, fitted black mini dress. Fisher takes a seat at the bar, waving for the bartender to come over. The young woman whispers into the other bartender's ear, and the bartender comes over to take Fisher's order.

"Can I have a Bacardi and Coke?" says Fisher. He then turns his attention to Symoné and Mike, who are on the dance floor. Symoné's an attractive, dark-skinned, young woman, with long legs, a big bust, and a tiny waist that makes her apple bottom butt appear bigger than it is. Symoné and Mike are dancing very close, sweating, and having a good time.

"Mike, I need something to drink. I'm hot and thirsty," Symoné says, and grabs Mike's hand, guiding him over to the bar.

"Two Cokes, please," Mike says.

The bartender places Fisher's drink on the bar. He picks up his drink, puts money on the bar, walks up behind Symoné, who's sitting at the other end with Mike, and taps her on the shoulder. She turns around and is shocked to see Fisher. "Hey, Jack. What you doing here?"

"I should be asking you that. Does your father know you're here?" Fisher asks.

"Ah . . . No. Not really."

Mike looks on, confused. He wonders who the man Symoné is talking with.

"I'm spending the night at a girlfriend's house. Please don't tell my father we came to this party."

"You have a ride home?"

"Yes."

"Jack, promise me you won't tell my father."

"Believe it or not, I was young once."

"Thank you, Jack," Symoné says and kisses him on the cheek. Fisher gets up and leaves.

"So, who was that?" Mike asks.

"My Godfather and father's partner, Detective Jack Fisher."

"Why didn't you introduce me?"

"Mike now is not a good time. I'm not even supposed to be in here. I swear, I hope he doesn't tell my father."

"You ready to go?" Mike asks.

"Yeah. Where's Chrissy? My stomach is bothering me."

Mike leaves money for the Cokes on the bar, and they leave without their drinks.

❊ ❊ ❊

It's a dreary afternoon, the Tuesday after Labor Day, in 1988. Heavy rains cascade through the thunder and lightning of a darkening sky. Wild winds scatter leaves into the air and onto the concrete. People start to run for shelter, desperately holding their umbrellas and hats. But the wind is too much.

During the evening shift change, the precinct's lobby is busy with plain clothes and uniformed officers. Detective Vaughn Harris is in his mid-fifties, but looks like he's in his late thirties. He wears a blue Yankees baseball cap and matching Starter jacket. He has a bouquet of flowers with a label attached that says, "Just because. Always your devoted husband Vaughn." He is surround by fellow officers, who make small talk and teasing remarks.

"Is that for me? Awwww, you didn't have to," a male officer says and reaches out to take the flowers.

"You wish. I knew you always wanted me," Harris responds and they bust out in laughter.

Harris was married to his high school sweetheart, Mae, with an eight-year-old daughter when he began his career with the NYPD in 1978 as a rookie, while also attending John Jay College of Criminal Justice part-time. Harris later became a member of the distinguished Pattern Identification Unit, which specializes in the apprehension of serial criminals. He graduated from the New York City Police Academy with the highest combined average for academics, physical achievement, and marksmanship. Two years later he received a B.A. in Criminology from John Jay College. He is a no-nonsense narcotics officer, who does what it takes to get the job done; always by the book and in total opposite of his partner and best friend, Detective Fisher.

Harris is charming and carries himself very well. Everyone is happy just by being around him. He is clean-cut and strikingly handsome for an older guy. He is also well built and stands at 6'2. His shoulders are wide and the muscles can be easily seen through his denim shirt. Despite his size, he is neither intimidating or uninviting. All of the officers, especially the rookies, go to him for answers and advice because he just seems to always have the answer. And the female officers go to him with their male problems because they know he is happily married and respectful.

The banter stops and the conversation gets serious.

"So you heard I.A. is doing random interviews. They're here at the precinct," a female office whispers.

"Yeah, I know. I'm being interviewed in a few," says Harris with a look of disgust.

The officers are wide-eyed and their mouths agape. "What?" they all say simultaneously with horrified looks on their faces.

"I'm good. I'm not worried," Harris says calmly.

"That's some bullshit," a rookie spits.

"The cleanest cop in the city " by far," another female officer retorts.

"Your partner on the other hand," a seasoned officer says with sarcasm.

Harris's body stiffens at the remark, even though he knows there's truth to it. However, still defends his partner and best friend, Fisher. "That's just station house gossip."

"If you say so," responds the seasoned officer.

Harris glances at his wristwatch and notices the time. "I to have go. I need to head on to this interview with I.A."

He walks off leaving the officers whispering in a huddle.

❋ ❋ ❋

The bending branches of a tall oak tree crash against the gated window of the precinct's conference room, which has been turned into a makeshift interrogation room. A large boat-shaped table is positioned in the middle of the room with three high-back, leather chairs. A tack board mounted on the conference room wall displays precinct memos, announcements, missing persons flyers, and job postings. A coffee table, setup with donuts and bagels, sits in the corner of the room next to a water cooler. Above the cooler hangs a picture of the Police Commissioner, Benjamin Ward.

Harris looks at his wristwatch and becomes agitated. He begins to fiddle with his shield, which hangs from a chain around his neck. He thinks to himself: *These fucking guys have me waiting like I have nothing better to do.*

The front door to the conference room swings open. In walk two Internal Affairs Bureau Investigators, Bobby Washington and Dennis Jones. Harris takes a deep breath and sits down.

Washington is an experienced I.A. investigator. He is bald with a thick, groomed salt and pepper mustache. The years of working the tough streets of New York City are etched in every line and wrinkle on his face. Washington is close to retirement and training Jones, the younger, more eager. investigator.

Washington heads over to the large window, where Harris was standing, and draws the curtains. Jones enters with a pep in his step and places a black leather briefcase on the table after he closes the door. He opens up the briefcase and sits.

Harris, now seated opposite Investigators Washington and Jones, waits patiently in silence as the investigators arrange files on the table. Jones takes a tape recorder out of the briefcase, puts it on the table, and hits the record button. He then confidently leans back in his chair with a pen and yellow notepad in his hand.

The silence in the room is broken, as Washington begins to explain to Harris the reason for the conference. "This is a formal interview of Detective Vaughn Harris, concerning allegations of corruption and civilian complaints of serious misconduct by Detective Jack Fisher, Harris's partner. Harris has been informed of his administrative rights before this interview, and understands the nature of this investigation, and the reason for this conference. Do you understand why you are here, Detective Harris?"

"Yes."

"And have you been informed of your administrative rights prior to this interview?"

Harris nods and answers for the tape recorder, "Yes."

"We will commence with the questioning of Harris's knowledge of his partner's alleged corruption and misconduct."

Jones leans back in his chair. He takes notes without breaking eye contact with Harris.

"How is your relationship with your partner?" asks Washington.

Harris answers the question with extreme confidence. "Good. Detective Fisher is my daughter's Godfather. But, we haven't spent much time together outside of work for a while."

"Godfather? So I wouldn't be foolish to assume you two keep no secrets from each other?" asks Washington with sarcasm in his voice.

"I hope not. Detective Fisher knows he can come and talk to me about anything," says Harris.

"Were you aware that your partner, Detective Fisher, was working for a known street pimp named Sweets?"

"No."

"According to informants, Detective Fisher was keeping the cops off Sweets's back and allowing Sweets to run a house of prostitution, with under-age girls in the back of his strip club, Sweet Cherry. The informant confirmed that Fisher took payoffs or was given access to young prostitutes in return."

"No, I was not aware."

"Do you remember responding to an Esser Baptiste noise complaint with Detective Fisher, Memorial Day Weekend, May 28, 1988, at the Lenox Terrace Apartment Complex on 135th Street?" asks Washington.

"Yeah, I remember Ms. Baptiste. Lil' West Indian woman with a very heavy accent. She tried to hit on me, and I told her I was happily married."

Washington sits up straight in his seat with a stern, this-is-not-a-joke expression on his face, and seriousness in his voice. "Well, according to Ms. Baptiste and a notice of claim filed by her attorney, your partner, Detective Fisher, came back to her home on several different occasions after that day. He used his badge to pressure her to date him. Then stalked her and ultimately threatened her with violence."

Harris is dumbfounded by what he hears, but keeps control of his emotions, so as not to reveal his true feelings. "I don't know anything about that. I have not seen or spoken with Ms. Baptiste again after that day."

Investigators Washington and Jones indiscreetly give each other an odd look. They are unable to read Harris's facial expressions and body language.

"Your partner's name also came up in another case in New Jersey, along with eight patrol officers charged with smuggling guns into the state." Washington continues, as he scans through documents on the table. "There is a long list of complaints and allegations against your partner." Washington shares this with hopes of breaking Harris down.

Washington begins to read off more allegations about Detective Fisher. "He helped some police officers plant drugs on people to meet arrest quotas. He was the lookout in the robbery of a perfume warehouse. We've got him down for beating suspects and extorting drug dealers." Washington looks at Harris dead on. "The list goes on."

Despite the shocking reveal, Harris begins to tune Washington out. His thoughts start to drift back to a conversation he had with his partner earlier in the year. He had heard the rumors around the precinct and even spoke with Fisher about some of the allegations. Fisher danced around the questions and made light of the rumors with jokes and would quickly change the subject. Now that he was being interrogated, Harris began to believe that these allegations against his partner were true.

Jones interjects with concern in his tone, "Why are you protecting him?"

Harris clears his thoughts. "I'm not protecting anyone," he says.

Washington bangs his hand on the conference table and raises his voice. "I don't believe you! Maybe you know more than you're saying."

"What!" Harris can no longer control his emotions. He gets up, puts his hands on the conference table, and leans in toward Washington, giving him direct eye contact. "Are you saying I'm a dirty cop?"

Jones stops taking notes and puts down the pen. He moves in closer to the table. "No. That's not what we're saying," he replies calmly.

"But you're not blind, Harris," Washington says in an agitated voice.

Harris takes his hands off the conference table and stands straight up. "I'm not talking anymore. I want to speak with my delegate."

Frustrated, Jones combs his hand through his hair, leans back into the chair, and sighs, "No problem."

Washington takes a deep breath, opens the conference room door for Harris, "You are free to go, but this is far from over. We will speak again."

❋   ❋   ❋

It's late in the evening, and the rain has finally slowed down. Detective Fisher pulls his unmarked police car, a burgundy Chevy Impala, in front of a two-story, red brick house in the suburbs of White Plains, New York. He parks and beeps his horn several times. The hanging porch light illuminates the entrance of the house. The landscape is well kept. A colorful garden of roses, daisies, lilies, and orchids run along the perimeter. The leaves of the autumn blaze pear trees that frame the house are turning red. The curved stone walkway extends from the street directly to the front steps of the house, where two wooden rocking chairs and a swing rest on the porch.

The front doors open and Symoné, appears. Dressed in a pair of denim shorts and a baby-doll t-shirt that exposes her flat belly, she runs down the walkway toward the car. Her large rollers bounce lightly as she makes her way toward Detective Fisher.

Detective Fisher sees Symoné running toward him and gets out of the car. He is drearily dressed in dark blue and black, with gray New Balance sneakers. He walks toward Symoné. A light wind blows the back of his windbreaker up and exposes his hand-held, two-way radio clipped to his belt, and a .38-caliber revolver tucked in the back of his waistband. Symoné runs up to Detective Fisher and gives him a hug and a kiss on the cheek.

"This is a big surprise. You haven't been by the house in a while," she says.

"Yeah, I've been working hard trying to keep the bad guys off the streets," he replies.

"Jack, you're not going to tell my father about me going to Sweet Cherry's, right?"

"Of course not, baby girl. Didn't I promise you? That's our little secret, okay."

"Okay." She squeezes him tight and plants another kiss on his cheek. "Jack, you're the best God-daddy any girl can ask for."

Detective Fisher smiles and takes Symoné's hand and slowly turns her around, checking out her young, fully developed body. "You're growing up, look at you. You're filling out into a fine, young woman, Symoné."

Symoné blushes, pulls her hand away, and starts to strike model-like poses. "You think so?" she asks coyly, with a smile on her face. She fiddles with the 18-carat, heart-shaped locket around her neck. "You know, I'm graduating high school this year. I wish daddy and mommy could see that and stop being so overprotective. Then I wouldn't have had to lie to them about going to Sweet Cherry. They treat me like a baby."

"I'll talk to them," he says.

"You promise?" she asks in a little girl voice.

"Yes, I promise," he confirms. Detective Fisher turns her around by the shoulders and gives her butt a slap. "Now hurry up and tell your dad I'm here. We have to go."

"Ouch," she says. She turns her head around and frowns at Detective Fisher. She looks baffled and uncomfortable. She hurries back up the walkway toward the house, yelling for her father. "DAD, JACK'S HERE!"

Detective Fisher follows behind her. He watches her butt as if in a trance, turning his head from side to side, with a lustful grin on his face. He nods his head, as if to offer her butt a stamp of approval. Symoné is oblivious to what is going on behind her. She reaches the porch and walks up the stairs. Detective Fisher stops at the front porch, leans against the stone column, and watches her go into the house. A few moments later Harris appears at the front door. He leans down and adjusts his jeans over the small Ruger in the ankle band holster. The bend of his body exposes the .38-caliber revolver in his cross harness, shoulder holster under his plaid button up.

Detective Fisher glances at Harris, then down at his wristwatch, and back at Harris. "It's ten o'clock, time is wasting, my man. We got to go," he says in a joking manner.

Harris sighs and says, "Yeah, I know."

Detective Fisher notices that Harris is not in a joking mood. Mae, comes to the door. She is an extremely attractive, older woman with an athletic built, and she is wearing a terry jumper that shows off her hourglass shape.

"Hey Fisher, how's it going?" she says with a big smile on her face.

"Damn Mae, every time I see you, you lookin' younger. Come here and give me a hug," he says, grabbing Mae's waist and kissing her on the cheek. Mae playfully pushes Detective Fisher away and laughs.

He looks at Harris and says teasingly, "You know this was supposed to be my wife, right?"

"Stop talking so much, man. Let's go," he retorts, and then turns to his wife. "Tell Symoné I thought about it and she can go with Mike to the movies this weekend."

A smile forms across Mae's face. She cradles her husband face between her hands, gazes into his eyes, and gives him a gentle peck on his lips.

Detective Fisher looks on with envy.

"She'll be happy to hear that," "She'll be happy to hear that the two's eyes."

Detective Fisher clears his throat. "Harris, we gotta go."

Harris plants another quick kiss on his wife's lips before she heads into the house. Harris and Fisher walk to the Chevy Impala. They get in and drive off into the night, down the dark suburban street.

MY BROTHER'S KEEPER

. . . .

CHAPTER 2

September 7, 1988

It's one o'clock in the morning, Detective Harris and Fisher cruise down the streets of Harlem. Harris is quiet and staring out the passenger side window.

Detective Fisher notices his partner's melancholy mood. "What's up with the silent treatment, man?"

"I got a lot on my mind, man, a lot on my mind," Harris responds.

Detective Fisher tries to make light of the situation and tries to cheer his partner up. "Well my man, I got food on my mind. Let's go to Willie Burgers and get something to eat before we head over to Dunbar."

"We need to talk, Jack," Harris says suddenly.

"Talk about what? What's going on?" Detective Fisher asks.

"I had a meeting with I.A. yesterday," Harris announces.

"I.A.?"

"Yeah, I.A."

"I'm listening." Detective Fisher starts chewing on the inside of his bottom lip.

"What's going on with you, Fisher?"

"What you mean?" Detective Fisher wants to know.

"Remember that noise complaint we responded to in Lennox Terrace?"

"You talking about that West Indian woman?"

"Yeah, Esser Baptiste," Harris replies.

"What about her?"

"You tell me, you saw her. Did you know she filed a complaint on your ass with the department?"

"Yeah, I know. That vindictive bitch! She got mad at me because I screwed her cousin. I couldn't help myself, the bitch was fine. Every time I came around, she was half dressed and all over me."

Harris is becoming irritated with Detective Fisher's nonchalant attitude and lack of concern with the Internal Affairs Bureau investigation. "Why you always thinking with the wrong head, man? What's happening with you? You've changed over the years."

"No, you changed," Detective Fisher snaps. "You're the one that got married and had a child."

"So whatever is going on, you blame me?"

"Nah, let's drop it. I already talked to Esser about the situation. She was a little upset, but she's gonna drop the charges."

"And what about Sweets, you moonlight for him now?"

"Yeah, money is money, my man. I got habits and women cost. I'm not married. What I.A. gon' do, arrest me for doing security at a strip club? You worry too much, man. I'm good." He pulls in front of Willie Burgers and parks.

"No, you are not good. I.A.'s comin' for you, man."

Detective Fisher's mobile phone rings. He answers the call. "Hey baby, hold on a minute." Detective Fisher opens the door, gets out, and asks, "You want something from Willie's?"

"Nah, I'm good."

Harris's face turns from annoyed to suspicious, as he watches his partner go up to the fast food joint. He rolls down his window and tries to eavesdrop on the conversation.

❊　❊　❊

Detective Fisher is now seated in the passenger side, eating his Willie burger. Harris shifts the Impala into gear and cruises to Adam Clayton Powell Jr. Boulevard, toward the Paul Laurence Dunbar Houses, known in the streets as "The Cave." It is a large, closed-in, brick complex, with several six-story walk-ups that occupy an entire city block, between 149th and

150th. It stretches across Adam Clayton Powell, Jr. to Frederick Douglass Boulevards.

Harris turns the corner onto 149th Street. Fisher notices Craig Little a.k.a. Little, a young, big-time drug dealer and captain of a notorious Harlem gang. He's talking with one of his soldiers, Caz, a tall, lanky Rasta with dreads. Caz is wearing a military style jacket and matching bucket hat. Nestled next to him is an around-the-way girl named Lola. Lola is a very attractive, young Puerto Rican, with long, black curly hair. Caz and Lola sit on the steps, in front of a boarded-up tenement, smoking weed and drinking beer.

Detective Fisher makes eye contact with Craig Little as they cruise into the block. Craig Little's clothes are without wrinkles and brand new. He wears a black Adidas tracksuit and matching Adidas shell tops. His accessories include black frame Cazals, black Kangol bucket hat, and a heavy gold rope chain. Craig Little watches the unmarked car turn onto Frederick Douglass Boulevard and head toward 150th Street. He removes his pager from the clip, and presses *50*, then turns to Caz. "I need you on alert in the Cave, a.s.a.p."

Caz nods his head, "Yeah mon." He takes out his thirteen-inch Italian switchblade and walks quickly out of sight, down the block, into one of the Dunbar vestibules on 149th Street.

Craig Little reaches into his pocket and hands over his car keys to Lola and says, "My 4Runner is on Adam Clayton Powell. Have the engine running. Be ready to move when I come out the Cave."

"I got you, papi," she says, winking. Craig Little makes another call and hurries in the opposite direction to Frederick Douglass.

150th Street appears empty and dimly lit by the few working street-lights. Harris pulls the Impala across the street from the Dunbar Complex. He parks behind some abandoned car, in front of burnt out tenements surrounded by scaffolding.

Detective Fisher finishes his Willie burger and gives his partner a perplexed look. He is wondering how much Harris knows, and if this is the same friend he grew up with in high school. Could he still trust Harris with his life or did Internal Affairs get to him? What if they were using his partner as a mule to get information? Detective Fisher knew Harris was a clean cop, who generally did things by the book. He wondered how long he would remain clam about his best friend being a dirty cop. It was just a matter of time before Internal Affairs came after him. Then he started to wonder how much the Internal Affairs Bureau had on him.

"So what else did I.A. talk about?" he asks, opening the glove compartment. From it, he pulls out a small silver flask. He unscrews the cap, takes a sip, and puts it back.

Harris takes a deep breath, looks his partner in the eyes, and says, "You being a dirty cop."

"What you mean?"

"Come on, Jack, we've been friends since high school. You think I'm that crazy?"

"Never that, my dude," Detective Fisher responds.

"I know shit been going on a long time, Jack. I chose not to see. Closed my eyes and looked the other way."

"But let me explain."

"Explain what? How you fucked up? Or how I just sat back and let this shit go on as long as I did, covering up for your ass, knowing the truth. Now I.A. tryna' drag my black ass into your bullshit."

"So what are you saying, Vaughn?"

"I love you like a brother, but you on your own with this one," he says and exits the unmarked car.

"Vaughn, what you mean?" Detective Fisher asks as he hurries to open the passenger side door.

"We don't have time for this now, we have a job to do. I'll take the Dunbar entrance on Adam Clayton and you take the entrance on 150th," Harris explains and then heads into the complex.

With ten different entryways in and out of the complex, the Dunbar is a criminal's escape paradise and a cop's nightmare. The courtyard garden inside has half-dead hedge plants and shrubs. Enormous trees with crooked leafy branches hover over the buildings and the entryways, making the complex dark and eerie.

Dobie, one of Craig Little's soldiers, is a short, dark-skinned, stone-faced, muscular man, with a well-groomed mustache and goatee. He's wearing a Carhartt jacket and Tims He exits building A and walks into the courtyard near the 150th entryway, carrying a large, black duffle bag over his shoulder. Willow is an enforcer and Craig Little's lieutenant. He is a tall, handsome, light-skinned guy, with an athletic build. He is bald and clean-shaven. Willow exits a few minutes after Dobie, carrying a sneaker box in a large Footlocker bag. Willow's pager is beeping on his waist side. The display reads *50*.

"Be ready. The block is hot," Willow warns Dobie. They take their 9mm Berettas from their waist and continue walking. They are unaware that Detective Fisher is watching them from inside the archway of the next building.

Detective Fisher takes his radio from the clip on his belt and whispers into it, "Fat Cat is on the move. Over."

"Ten-Four," Harris responds. "What's your location? Over."

"Courtyard. Over," Detective Fisher answers.

"Ten-Four. Over and out," Detective Harris says.

"Over and out," Detective Fisher replies, stepping out of the archway. "Excuse me, fellas. Can I talk to ya for a second?" Willow and Dobie recognize Detective Fisher as five-o and immediately begin shooting at him. They take cover, running in separate directions. Detective Fisher bolts backs into the archway.

Craig's soldier, Caz, emerges from the vestibule at 149th Street, with his switchblade ready and proceeds into the courtyard. He sees Willow and Dobie running and firing their guns. Caz sneaks back into the vestibule, peeks out, and waits for the right time to make his move.

Dobie runs out of the 150th Street exit. Willow attempts to run out the Adam Clayton Powell exit. Detective Fisher shoots a warning shot into the air. "STOP OR I WILL SHOOT!" When the drug dealers don't obey, Fisher lets off another shot, grazing Willow in the arm.

Willow grabs his arm and stops running. He is trapped in the vestibule entryway at the Adam Clayton Powell exit. He throws down his gun, drops the Footlocker bag, and puts his hand into the air, struggling to raise his injured arm.

"Turn around, put your hands up against the wall, and kick the gun over here," Detective Fisher demands, with his eyes and gun trained on

Willow. He reaches down, picks up the suspect's gun, and tucks it into his front pant waist.

"Ain't you gon' read me my rights?" asks Willow.

"You have the right to shut the FUCK UP. Now where's the money?" Detective Fisher exclaims.

Willow turns his head and spits on the ground near Detective Fisher's foot. Detective Fisher looks around to see if anyone is watching, unaware that Caz is peeking out the vestibule archway and sees everything. Detective Fisher hits Willow in the head with the butt of his gun. Willow crashes into the wall, holding his head. Blood is running down his face. Detective Fisher puts his gun away, picks up the Footlocker bag, and opens the box inside.

"Well, well, what do we have here?" he says, pleased. Detective Fisher pulls out stacks of hundreds and twenties, wrapped with rubber bands.

"Oh, so that's how it is, huh?" Willow says, as he wipes the blood from his eyes. He sees Caz creeping out the vestibule archway, walking carefully up the walkway toward him and the undercover detective.

"Face that wall and shut the fuck up before I shoot your ass again," Detective Fisher says.

Willow complies and turns to the wall with a sinister smile on his face. Detective Fisher lifts up his pant leg and starts stuffing stacks into his socks, unaware of the danger he is in with Caz sneaking up behind him.

Detective Harris enters the vestibule with his gun drawn and peeks out of the archway. He sees his partner taking the drug money and is stunned. With his gun still in his hand, he wipes the sweat from his forehead and continues to move slowly into the vestibule.

"Fisher, what you doing?" he asks, his gun drawn.

Willow lifts his head and sees Detective Harris.

"I . . ." Detective Fisher is speechless and puts his head down.

"Cat got your tongue, huh?" Willow says.

Willow and Detective Harris see Caz approaching. Detective Fisher's back is turned and he is unaware of the danger he is in. Detective Harris aims his gun at Caz.

Detective Fisher lifts his head and sees his partner aiming in his direction. He quickly grabs Willow's 9mm that's tucked in the front of his pants waist. He aims it at Detective Harris. Willow quickly moves out of harm's way. In the blink of an eye, the sounds of two gunshots fill the air. BOOM, BOOM! Detective Harris is shot in the head and falls to the ground. Willow steps over Detective Harris's body and escapes through the Adam Clayton Powell exit.

❋ ❋ ❋

Detective Fisher checks his body to see if he has been shot, then turns and sees Caz behind him, lying motionless on the ground with a switchblade open in his hand. He puts the gun back into his waist, runs over to his partner, and tries to stop the bleeding by applying pressure to the gunshot wound. Detective Harris is bleeding heavily from his head. Blood is everywhere. He takes a deep breath and dies.

Detective Fisher is in shock, but quickly snaps out of it. He takes a handkerchief out of his pocket and wipes his fingerprints off the 9mm. He is so preoccupied with covering up the shooting he does not see Craig Little in the courtyard, watching him at a distance.

Detective Fisher walks over to Caz's dead body and puts Caz's fingerprints on the 9mm used to murder his partner, Detective Harris. He removes the switchblade from Caz's hand and puts it into his pocket, then calls in the shooting on his radio. "Ten-thirteen . . . officer down. Ten-thirteen. . . officer down."

It starts to rain. Craig Little exits the Dunbar through the Frederick Douglass Boulevard exit, where his 4Runner is waiting.

❋ ❋ ❋

A week after Detective Harris's murder, he is given an Inspector's Funeral, held in honor of officers who die in the line of duty. There are hundreds of officers in attendance. They all wear black bands across their shields. There are a few officers with watery eyes, while others try and hold back tears, all lined up outside the Riverside Church in Harlem. Civilian mourners dressed in t-shirts with Officer Harris's picture, curious passersby, community leaders, and residents have all come to pay their respects. Internal

Affairs Investigators Washington and Jones are also at the funeral, taking mental notes and blending in with the crowd.

Loudspeakers are setup outside, affording those who are unable to fit into the crowded sanctuary the chance to listen to the proceedings. The Police Commissioner's voice rings over the loudspeakers. "We owe Detective Vaughn Harris's family our deepest sympathy, our everlasting loyalty, and a total accounting of the facts. Vaughn was a police officer first, last, and always."

In perfect formation, the first to exit the church are the police escorts, next to the Bishop and clergymen, followed by six officers carrying Detective Harris's metallic blue casket, which is covered with a green and white police flag. Mae, Symoné, Detective Fisher, and Mike, exit the church behind Detective Harris's casket. The casket is hoisted into a waiting hearse, as a bugler plays taps. The loud noise of police helicopters circulates overhead in missing-man formation.

Mae has a black shawl over her shoulders. She is wearing a black, flat-brimmed hat, a long sleeved dress, a black veil, and sunglasses. Detective Fisher is in his dress uniform with his arms around Mae, trying to console her. Symoné is wearing a black sleeveless dress, button-up black sweater, and holding tight to the heart-shaped locket hanging from her neck, that her father had given her. She releases the locket to clutch her mother's hand and uses the other to wipe the tears from her face. Mike is neatly dressed in a dark tailored suit, blue shirt, and paisley tie. He stands by Symoné's side and tries to comfort her with an occasional hug and soft back rub.

Doves are released, as the chief of police approaches Mae on the church steps and presents her with a flag. She takes the flag, grips it tightly to her chest, and breaks down in tears. Detective Fisher puts his arms around Mae and pulls her close. She lets go of Symoné's hand, buries her face in Detective Fisher's chest, and cries. The expression on Symoné's face shows her displeasure with their display of affection.

1989

LOST INNOCENCE

. . . .

CHAPTER 3

The Harris's Home, February 10, 1989

Months after Detective Vaughn Harris's murder, Detective Fisher has slowed down his illegal activities due to the Internal Affairs Bureau Investigation. He has been helping Mae around the house and through her grief. He is a temporary guest that has made himself quite comfortable in his deceased partner's home.

Fisher is stretched out in the living room, on the cozy leather sofa, with his feet on the coffee table. He is drinking a Heineken and watching a football game on the TV.

Symoné walks into the living room, wearing her cut-off daisy-duke shorts. A hair clip is keeping her messy bun in place as she carries a large glass and plate. Wires from Walkman headphones dangle from her ears. Her head stops nodding to the music when she notices Fisher's feet on the table. Annoyed, she slides the headphones around her neck.

"Jack, you know if my mom's working late tonight? I'm trying to go out."

"Yeah, she called. The night nurse is running late."

Symoné sucks her teeth and rolls her eyes. "She always works late."

"Isn't it kind of late for you to be going out?"

"I'm not a baby, Jack. I'm a big girl, and it's Friday. There's no school tomorrow."

"Excuse me, miss I'm grown now."

Symoné goes into the kitchen. Fisher watches her with eager eyes. He feels his manhood throbbing as it starts rising. He looks down at his pants, picks up one of the throw pillows, and covers the evidence of his arousal.

Symoné walks out of the kitchen and heads upstairs to her bedroom. She does not notice Fisher watching her. He gets up, adjusts his aching bulge from its uncomfortable position, turns up the TV, and follows Symoné.

The door to Symoné›s bedroom is closed. Fisher knocks. There is no answer. He opens the door and walks in. Posters of R&B and Rap artists cover the walls. A pale yellow canopy bed, with a matching desk and dresser and attached mirror, furnish the room. The dresser is covered with antique dolls and a jewelry box with a ballerina carousel that plays music. On the nightstand is a large, double picture frame of Symoné in her cheerleader uniform and Mike, in his basketball uniform, holding a trophy. An oversized Valentine›s Day card, a red teddy bear, a vase with partially wilted red roses, and a heart-shaped candy box are very telling of the couple›s young love.

Symoné is sitting on the edge of the bed, painting her toenails, listening to the music blasting from her headphones. Occasionally, she glances at the music videos on the TV above the mini wall unit, which is filled with her cheerleading trophies and awards. Her back is turned to the door, and she does not see or hear Fisher enter the room. He walks closer to the bed and touches her shoulder. Symoné is startled. She takes off the headphones and quickly turns around.

"Dag Jack, you scared me. Now I messed up my pedicure."

"I knocked on the door," he admits and sits on the bed next to Symoné. "So, what's going on? Looking forward to graduation?"

"Yeah, for sure. I'm tired of school."

Fisher reaches across Symoné, purposely brushing up against her young, firm breasts, to pick up the picture frame with the photo of her and Mike. "So, this is the lucky guy I saw you with in Sweet Cherry?"

"Yep," she says, continuing to paint her toenails.

Fisher puts the picture frame on the bed, goes into his pocket, and pulls out a blunt. He lights the blunt, takes two puffs, and taps Symoné on the shoulder. Symoné turns around, surprised to see her Godfather smoking weed.

"I won't tell, if you don't," he says and puts the blunt up to her lips.

Symoné hesitates a moment, then takes the blunt from Fisher and smokes. She chokes and coughs. Fisher laughs, taking the blunt from Symoné and puts it out on the picture frame. He begins to pat and rub Symoné's back. She falls back onto the bed, laughing and coughing.

Symoné's beauty and voluptuous breasts arouse Fisher. He leans over Symoné and fondles her breast. Symoné knocks his hands away and attempts to get up from the bed. Fisher pushes her back onto the bed and pins her down under his powerful muscular frame. She struggles to get from under Fisher, slapping and scratching at his arms and face. The glass picture frame crashes to the floor, shattering.

"Get off me. I can't breathe."

Fisher ignores Symoné pleads. Like a savage, he tears off her top, exposing her breast. The chain with the heart-shaped locket breaks, falling to the floor. He grabs her petite wrists with one hand and holds them above her head, as he unfastens his belt and zips his pants with the other. She continues to struggle to break free of his grip, but he is twice her size and too strong. She sees his swollen manhood and struggles desperately to break free.

"STOP PLEASE! JACK STOP!" she says and begins to cry.

She is exhausted, but still tries to fight Fisher off. He rips the crotch of her shorts open, entering her fully in one deep thrust. She cries out in pain. He covers her mouth.

"Forgive me," he says breathing heavily. He smothers her face with sloppy, wet kisses. His goatee felt like steel wool on her soft skin. He tries to force her sealed lips open with his hot slimy tongue. He roughly palms her bare breasts with his callused hands, sucking and squeezing them tight. His body is wet and sweaty, and he reeks of alcohol. His musty sweat drips onto her face and into her mouth, making her gag. She screams and cries louder. Her pleas for mercy fell on deaf ears. The more she screams, the more turned on Fisher becomes, thrusting into her in a fierce paroxysm. Symoné passes out underneath Fisher. In a harsh groan of masculine satisfaction, he releases himself inside her and falls limp onto her lifeless body.

Moments later, Symoné wakes to find Fisher sitting on the bed, wiping her face and forehead with a cold cloth. She knocks the cloth from his hand.

"GET OUT, GET OUT!" she screams, grabbing the spread on the bed to cover her body.

"Symoné, I'm sorry. I don't know what came over me – you're so beautiful. I couldn't help myself," he tries to explains.

"GET OUT!"

"Calm down. Calm down, Symoné, and listen," he says and tries to touch her arm. Symoné pulls away and balls up at the headboard of her bed.

"NO! GET OUT NOW!"

Fisher slowly gets up from the bed and continues to plead with Symoné. "You're not going to tell your mother, right? I swear I'll make this up to you. I promise. Please don't tell your mother," he begs as he turns to leave her bedroom, closing the door behind him.

Symoné is in a great deal of pain and struggles to get off the bed. She grabs the damp cloth and gets up, leaving a trail of blood smeared on the bed. She limps over to the mirror, holding on to the dresser. She takes the damp cloth and wipes off her legs and thighs. She lifts her hand and stares into the mirror for a long time. *An image appears that looks like her, but the reflection she sees is a girl covered with dirt; she is frail and worn down.* Symoné takes the damp cloth and starts to scrub her face rigorously, her neck and then her arms; over and over again, scrubbing her body raw.

❊ ❊ ❊

Mae looks exhausted as she enters the house. She slowly walks over to the sofa, plops down with her coat still on and pocketbook in hand. She takes off her nurse shoes and rubs her sore feet. She looks over at the end table and sees an old family photo with her, Symoné, and her husband, Vaughn. She goes to pick it up and smiles. Mae then grabs her shoes and pocketbook and notices light coming from underneath the door of the guest room. She knocks.

"Come in," the voice says on the other side.

Mae opens the door and finds Fisher pulling clothes out of the dresser draw, packing his suitcase.

"Where you going?" she asks, standing at the doorway.

"I'm heading out in the morning, I think I've overstayed my welcome and you appear to be adjusting much better since Vaughn's death. You don't need me anymore."

"Yes, I do need you." she replies, putting her bag and shoes down next to Fisher's suitcase. Mae starts taking the clothes out of the suitcase and puts them back into the drawers. Fisher stands there, watching Mae unpack his suitcase. He is nervous and begins to sweat. He pulls out a handkerchief and wipes his forehead.

"Its been hard, for me and Symoné since Vaughn's murder. Having you around is comforting and makes me feel safe," she assures him, as she unpacks the last of his clothes.

"At least let me start giving you a few dollars to help out with some of the bills ." He reaches into his pocket and pulls out a few hundred-dollar bills, putting them in Mae's hand. She hands him back the money and kisses him on the cheek.

"I'll see you in the morning." She picks her things up and leaves the room.

Mae heads up the stairs to Symoné's bedroom. She quietly opens the door and peeks in. Symoné is in the bed, peeking out from under the covers and gripping a knife in her hand. She is sniffling, with tears falling down her face. The bedroom door opens, and she sees the light coming from the cracked door. She keeps very quiet and still.

"Symoné, you up?" Mae asks.

Symoné pretends not to hear her mother calling, but relived that she is home. Mae backs out of the room and softly closes the door behind her.

✳ ✳ ✳

Weeks after the rape, Symoné is having recurring nightmares. Symoné is in her canopy bed, tossing, turning, and mumbling in her sleep. The only light in the room is coming from the TV. Rain is coming down hard, hitting and bouncing off the window ledge. The ghostly sound of a strong wind can be heard outside the open window. The fierce wind blows the bedroom curtains in and out of the window. The sound of thunder, then a flash of lightning fills the bedroom. Symoné sits up abruptly. She wraps her hands around her shoulders and arms to shield herself from the cold breeze that has entered the room. Wide-eyed and breathing rapidly, she looks fearfully around the room.

Now realizing the storm outside, Symoné hurries out of bed and grabs her robe. She rushes over to the window, pulling in the wet curtains and shutting the window. She starts to gag and runs bent over toward the wastebasket in the corner of the bedroom, holding her stomach and mouth. She falls to the ground, grabs the wastebasket with both hands, and buries her face into it and vomits. When she is done, she feels faint and weak. She grabs hold of the dresser and pulls herself up. Face to face with her reflection in the mirror, she starts to cry.

❋ ❋ ❋

The curtains are open in Symoné's bedroom. The rays from the sunrise hit Symoné's face, as she lies asleep in her bed. She opens her eyes slightly and is bothered by the sun's presence. She closes her eyes, pulling the blanket over her head and tries to go back to sleep. The door to Symoné's bedroom opens. Mae enters the room, dressed in her nurse's uniform.

"Symoné, it's time to get up," she says.

Symoné does not move. Mae walks over and pulls the blanket off Symoné. Symoné pulls the blanket back over her head. Mae pulls it back down.

"Symoné, it's after seven. It's time to get up and out of bed. Let's go," Mae repeats.

Symoné rises, sleepy-eyed and groggy. "I'm tired and don't feel well."

"What's the matter, you have your period?" Mae asks.

"No, I just don't feel well," Symoné replies.

"Child, once you get up, wash-up, and have some breakfast, you'll be all right. I'm going in early this morning; one of the girls called in sick. There are some salmon cakes and home fries in the oven." Mae kisses Symoné on the forehead and leaves the room. Symoné pulls the blanket back over her head.

❋ ❋ ❋

An hour later Symoné comes down the stairs, dressed in her catholic school uniform. She stops at the kitchen›s entrance and observes the mess. She has bags under her eyes from lack of sleep and a nauseated look on her face. The kitchen sink is full of dishes. There are dirty pots on the stove and the trashcan is full. She shuffles over to the sink and begins to wash the dishes.

The wall telephone in the kitchen rings. She stops washing the dishes and grabs the phone. "Hello... Hi Mike," she says. "Of course I'm looking forward to the prom."

Fisher comes into the kitchen wearing a robe and plaid pajama bottoms. He glances over at Symoné on the telephone, then opens the refrigerator, takes out the orange juice, and pours himself a glass. He starts to drink and eavesdrops on Symoné's conversation.

"Mike, I have to go. I'll see you after practice," she says and hangs up the telephone. She removes the plate with salmon cakes, home fries, scrambled eggs, and cheese left by her mother in the oven. She sits at the table in the dining room and tries to eat. There are books on the table and a backpack is hanging from the chair she is sitting in.

Fisher brings his glass of orange juice into the dining area and joins Symoné at the table.

"Good morning," he says casually.

Symoné takes a deep breath and sighs.

"So, who were you talking to? Mike? Looking forward to prom night, huh?"

Symoné continues to ignore Fisher. She stops eating and stares down at her plate. She slowly pushes the food around with the fork. She opens a schoolbook and pretends to read.

"So, how long do you plan on giving me the silent treatment?" he asks, reaching over and gently touching her hand. She quickly pulls her hand away. "Symoné, how many times do I have to say I'm sorry? I messed-up. I know you may not care, but I told your mother I'll help with the prom expenses. Pay for whatever dress and shoes you want, as well as the limo." He gets up from the table and leaves.

Symoné watches Fisher walk away from the table with hatred in her eyes, and then gathers her books. She picks up her open backpack. A Planned Parenthood brochure falls out onto the parquet floor. She picks it up and puts it back into her bag, along with the books from the table. She empties the food into the trashcan and hurries out of the door.

PROM QUEEN
. . . .

CHAPTER 4

May 5, 1989

Prom night. Mike is sitting on the sofa with Fisher, who is reading a newspaper. Resting in a plastic case in the palm of his hand is a mini orchid corsage, to match the orchid pinned to the lapel of his Ralph Lauren tuxedo. Fisher pretends to read, as he looks at the handsome, young man from the side. He observes his laced-up gator shoes, diamond studs in both ears, a high school championship ring, and a stainless steel Rolex watch.

"I've been reading about you in the papers. You doin' big things, Mike," Fisher comments.

"Yeah," Mike says.

"Decided on a college yet?" Fisher asks.

"I got a few offers. I'm just waiting for that letter from UNC."

"Good team."

"HEY GUYS, HERE SHE COMES!" Mae announces from the top of the stairs.

Mike and Fisher stand up. Mike walks over to the bottom of the stairs and waits for Symoné. She looks stunning, like a princess, coming down the stairs in a short, strapless, peach ball gown and matching satin pumps. Her hair is elegantly swept up with crystal embellishments, which accent her diamond tennis bracelet and matching ring.

Symoné reaches the bottom of the staircase and Mae is behind her, snapping pictures of Mike's reaction.

"Wow, you look really nice," Mike says. He takes out the corsage and puts it on Symoné's wrist.

"What you think, Fisher, doesn't she look beautiful?" Mae exclaims.

"She sure does, Mae," Fisher replies while 'reading' his paper.

Mae takes several pictures of Mike and Symoné.

"Mom, could we please go now?" Symoné asks.

"All right, now, Mike, you drive carefully and don't be speeding," Mae says.

"Okay, Mrs. Harris," Mike replies.

Mike opens the door to the silver Benz and Symoné gets in. Mike gets in the driver's seat and they pull off. Mae stands at the door and watches the car until it is out of sight. Her eyes water and tears fall from her face. She smiles and goes back into the house.

❈ ❈ ❈

The music is loud at the prom after-party in the presidential suite at the Marriott Marquis. Mike's older brother, Eddie Blackwell, a.k.a. "Nice", is hosting it. ("Nice" is a big-time drug dealer in Harlem that got his nickname because of his skills on the basketball court. He had a promising career in the NBA, but was derailed after their mother died in a tragic hit-and-run accident.)

The DJ is playing Guy's, "Groove Me". Mike and Symoné are having fun and breaking it down on the dance floor. Many of Mike's friends pass by, showing them lots of love and thanking Mike for inviting them. Eddie and, Chrissy, interrupt Mike and Symoné.

"So what's good, baby brother? Having a good time?" Eddie asks and gives him a man-handshake and tight hug.

"Hey Mike," Chrissy says.

"Hey Chrissy, nice dress," Mike says.

"Thanks. Now can I borrow my homegirl for a while?" Chrissy asks and takes Symoné's hand, leaving Mike and Eddie to admire them as they walk off into the crowd. "Where you been hiding, girl?" Chrissy asks, as they hurry toward the bar. Symoné turns to wave bye to Mike.

The suite is jam packed with Mike's teammates and other graduating seniors are sweating it up, dancing all over the spacious living room. The aroma from the weed fills the suite. Some couples are making out on the sofas and chairs. The bartenders are busy pouring free, top shelf liquor and champagne for the underage drinkers, their tip jars filled to the rim.

"Could we have two champagne glasses and a bottle of Dom?" Chrissy asks the bartender, and then turns to Symoné, looking her up and down. "Damn girl, that dress and those shoes look cute on you, I picked out for Mike."

"So, you picked this out. I thought so. Yeah it's cute, that's why you my girl," Symoné says and then gives Chrissy a hug and kiss on her cheek. "Thank you. And as always, Eddie have you right; that Gucci dress and shoes you have on, are all that girl."

"Shit, I put enough work in, if you know what I mean. So how have you been doing? I haven't seen you since your dad passed," Chrissy says.

"Yeah, I've been hanging in there. I just wish my dad was here," Symoné replies.

"You know I am always here if you need to talk."

"I know," Symoné says and gets very serious. "Can I trust you? I mean really trust you?"

"Of course you can. I'm insulted that you feel the need to ask," Chrissy says.

"My dad's partner been staying at the house and . . ." Symoné says before being cut off by the bartender.

"Two glasses and your bottle of Dom."

"Thank you," Chrissy smiles and puts twenty dollars in the tip jar. "Now, hold that thought, Symoné. Let's toast to a good night and the loss of your virginity!"

Chrissy pops the bottle, pours the bubbly into the glass, and they drink. Symoné is bumped from behind by Kharizma, the captain of her high school cheerleading squad, and spills some of the champagne down the front of her dress.

"Oh, excuse me, my bad. Long time no see, Symoné," Kharizma says. She is with another cheerleader, GiGi. They both have sly grins on their faces.

"Bitch, you did that on purpose. My bad, my ass," Chrissy exclaims.

"What you say, Chrissy?" Kharizma snaps.

Symoné steps between Kharizma and Chrissy. "Chrissy, it's not that serious, and I don't want to spoil Mike's party," Symoné says.

"Symoné, you've missed a few practices, is everything okay?" Kharizma asks, as she rolls her eyes at Chrissy.

"Yeah, I'm good."

"So I'll see you at the next practice?"

"Yeah, I'll be there," Symoné says.

Kharizma looks Chrissy up and down and rolls her eyes again, before her and GiGi walk off in Mike's direction.

"That bitch be buggin'. She wants Mike so bad . . . you really need to check that bitch," Chrissy spits.

"I'm not worried about Mike," Symoné replies, as she watches Kharizma grab Mike's hand, pulling him. She starts dancing with him seductively. Mike sees Symoné and Chrissy watching him and moves back every time Kharizma tries to grind her ass on him.

"This is some party Eddie gave Mike. It must have cost him an arm and two legs. What kind of work does Eddie do?" Symoné asks.

"I don't know, never asked. Whatever it is, just keep the expensive gifts coming," Chrissy says. They laugh.

Mike and Eddie sneak up on them. Mike grabs Symoné from behind and kisses her on the neck. "What ya'll ladies over here gossiping about?"

"I don't gossip," Chrissy says.

"Yeah right, come on, we outta here," Eddie says to Chrissy. He helps her put on her silk wrap, kisses Symoné on the cheek, gives Mike a pound, and leaves. The DJ has just slowed the music down and plays, "Shower Me With Your Love" by Surface. Mike starts singing to Symoné, "My heart is filled with so much love. And I need, Symoné Harris to call my own. To fall in love, that's what everyone's dreaming of, I hold this feeling, oh, so strong. Life is too short to live alone . . ." He gently takes Symoné by the hand and escorts her to the dance floor. They slow dance, as Mike continues to sing in her ear.

❋ ❋ ❋

Hours later, the party guest have all gone home. Mike is in the presidential suite's master bedroom, lying across the king size bed with his shoes off. His suit pants are still on and his tuxedo shirt is unbuttoned, revealing his crispy, white tank top, his chiseled chest and broad shoulders. He is watching the TV and stops when Symoné comes out of the master bathroom, with a towel wrapped around her glistening wet body and her prom dress in her hand. Mike is captivated by her beauty and watches Symoné, walk over to the long, leather ottoman, where she lays the dress neatly across, then walks over to him and sits on the bed. He sits up and moves closer to Symoné.

"Symoné, are you sure you're ready to do this?" Mike asks.

"Mike, you've been waiting a long time for this. All the gifts, this beautiful dress, this night has been so special," Symoné says.

"You deserve the best," he replies.

"Sometimes I think you're just too good for me. I've been so difficult lately," she says. "I ..."

Mike interrupts Symoné. "Symoné, it's understandable. You just lost your father. I'm cool."

"I love you so much, Mike. If you only knew how much."

"Yeah, I love you too. I just don't want you to feel pressured into doing something you're not ready for. I can wait. I'm not going anywhere," he promises.

Symoné leans over and kisses Mike gently on the lips. "I love you no matter what happens, just remember that," she whispers.

"Is something supposed to happen? Do you plan on going somewhere?"

"No, I'm just saying."

He smiles and kisses Symoné and puts his arms around her shoulder. "You're shaking."

"I'm okay. I'm just a little scared. It's our first time together, and I don't want to disappoint you," she admits.

"Symoné. Stop worrying so much, it's okay," he says, gazing into her eyes.

Symoné gently lies back on the bed, as Mike delicately peels the towel off. Symoné is tense. she tries to shield her body, using her hands.

"Relax, its okay. Why you hidin', you're body is perfect," he assures her and tenderly pulls them away. His lips slowly move to meet hers. She closes her eyes and slightly parts her lips. He slides his tongue into her mouth makes sweeping, swirling motions and she follows his lead.

She can smell the sweet citric scent of Drakkar Noir on his body. It is pleasing to her senses. It relaxes her and she allows him to freely probe her body with his tongue. He gingerly suckles on her hardened black pearls and she responds with a shallow moan. He makes his way down between her thighs, where she is moist and soft. The sweet scent of her fiery furnace is intoxicating and awakens his flesh, making him eager to taste her.

Symoné feels like she is on fire. She feels a heat between her legs like never before. Her moans grow louder.

"Oh my God, Mike," she cries out and lifts her hips upward and pushes his head down. Suddenly, she is seized by a rush of sensation so intense her entire body tremors in ecstasy.

He raises his head from her center and sees a look of pure bliss on her face.

"Mike, just hold me please," she says, pulling him up.

He lays on her and they share a long embrace, then a passionate kiss. She can feel his manhood through his clothes on her inner thigh. She can't help but feel aroused again.

Mike can no longer contain himself. He is overcome with emotion – he needs her. He quickly pulls off his clothes and she helps.

He whispers into her ear. "I love you, Symoné."

She answers back. "I love you, more."

He positions himself on top of her. Gently, he rubs the tip of his member over the lips of her womanhood. He can feel the dampness between her thighs. Slowly, he enters her with only the head of his manhood. He can see the tears start to form in Symoné's eyes and stops.

"Are you okay?" he asks as he leans over to kiss away the tears.

She nods. "Yes."

He continues to guide himself inch by inch into her heated core. His large, swollen member becomes too much for her and she cries out in pain.

"I'm sorry, Symoné." Carefully, Mike pulls out, feeling the tightness of Symoné's core. He grits his teeth. She feels so good.

At once Symoné feels empty and reaches out toward his manhood and places it back at the door of her femininity. He groans. She exhales as he enters her tight, wet womanhood. She feels herself expand. After a few minutes it starts to feel good.

Mike gyrates in slow circles. His rhythm increases as Symoné's moans grow louder. She can feel his heart beat against her warm, tingling flesh. His breathing becomes unsteady. She arches toward him to take him further and to meet his next powerful thrust.

"Damn, Symoné, I love you so much."

"Oh, Mike."

The rhythm of his hips is fast and frantic. She continues to meet his thrusts. He is finally ready to succumb to pleasure. There's a sudden pulsing moment of release and her core tightens around him.

"YESSSSSSSSSSSSSSSS," he cries out and allows his molten juices to intermingle with hers.

And they fall asleep in each other arms.

MY BABY'S DADDYS

· ·

CHAPTER 5

May 26, 1989

    Mike lives with his brother, Eddie in Esplanade Gardens on 147th and Adam Clayton Powell, Jr. Boulevard in Harlem. In the living room of their black and white bachelor pad, a three-piece Italian sofa points toward an entertainment unit. Framed black and white photos (some of them autographed) of sports legends fill the walls. There is a Thriller in Manila photo of Muhammad Ali and Joe Frazier on the wall, as well as a photo of Tommie Smith and John Carlos at the 1968 Olympics, with their heads bowed and fists lifted. Joe Louis, Jackie Robinson, Satchel Page, and Jesse Owens all lent their greatness to the room. In the corner of the living room, a show case display of autographed sports memorabilia; gloves worn by Mike Tyson, Jim Brown's autographed football, Darryl Strawberry autographed home-run baseball, a pair of black and red Air Jordan 1's, Michael Jordan's first sneaker, and an original pair of 1923 Chuck Taylor All-Stars.

    Eddie is dressed in a Gucci sweat suit and matching sneakers. He sits on the sofa, watching Mike's taped regional title game with his best friend and lieutenant, Hershey; an extremely dangerous, attractive, and dark-skinned man, with a pleasant smile and perfect, pearly whites. They are in full swing, counting stacks of money on the coffee table.

    Mike enters the room, dressed in his catholic school uniform, and picks up the cordless phone on the coffee table. He's quickly distracted by his basketball game playing on the TV. The tape is at the moment when he hits the game-winning, three-point basket. He does a play-by-play of the action like an announcer, "Love crosses the front court, looks for help and finds Parker, Parker slips, passes back to Blackwell. Two seconds left on the clock. Blackwell drives across and over into a step back, pulls up for three, YES! It's good and the crowd goes wild!"

Eddie looks on at his brother proudly. Hershey smiles and shakes his head. "Boy, you crazy."

Mike runs over to the corner of the living room, grabs the basketball off the floor, and relives the game's winning play. "Heads-up!" he says and throws the ball to Eddie.

Eddie drops the stack of money he's counting all over the floor and catches the ball. "Com'on, Mike, stop playing. You see I'm counting this cheddar."

Hershey laughs, showing his pearly whites. "You slipping, Nice – getting old and losing your handling skillz."

"Never that," Eddie responds as he gets up, grabs the basketball and does some fancy dribbling. Mike smirks as he looks on at his big brother showing off.

"Okay, you still got a little something," Hershey admits, with sarcasm in his tone. "Now com'on, Kareem Abdul-Jabbar, let's finish countin' these stacks so we can get out of here."

Eddie rolls the ball off his hand and gets back to counting the money. Mike walks over to the closet and takes out his jacket and backpack. He pulls out an envelope from his backpack and hands it to Eddie and watches him read.

Eddie looks up at his brother, takes the letter out of the envelope, and reads aloud.

Dear Mike Blackwell,

Congratulations on your outstanding display of basketball talent this past year. Our staff at the University of North Carolina would like to express our sincere interest in you as a prospective student-athlete and inform you of our desire to recruit you.

"Congrats, Baby Nice," Hershey says.

Eddie is overcome with excitement, stops reading, jumps up, and embraces Mike, lifting him off the floor. "YOU GOT IN! YOU GOT IN!

MIKE NICE! YOU A TAR HEEL NOW! HELL YEAH!" he exclaims and falls back on the sofa, looking at the letter. His mood changes and he becomes gloomy. "Damn, I wish mom was still here. She'd be so proud of you."

"Yeah, but it's not like dad can't be here." Mike looks over at Hershey for some support. "Right, Hershey?"

"That's between you and your brother, Mike. I'm out of this one."

"FUCK THAT NIGGA! WHAT DA HELL HE EVER DID FOR US? I HELPED MOM RAISE YOU! I HELPED MOM PUT FOOD ON OUR TABLE, WHILE HIS ASS WAS OUT CHEATIN' WITH SOME TRICK!"

Mike takes a seat on the oversized love seat near the sofa and looks at his brother. "So you gonna be mad at him for the rest of your life?"

"I don't want to talk about it," Eddie concludes and takes a roll of money from his pocket. He puts it into Mike's hand. "I'm out, got some business to handle." Eddie hugs Mike, puts the shoeboxes full of money into a shopping bag, and him and Hershey are out the door.

Mike remains seated on the sofa with a concerned look on his face, as he watches Eddie leave. He picks up the University of North Carolina interest letter, looks at it, and smiles.

❋   ❋   ❋

The elevator doors open, and Symoné sees a crowded waiting area in the Planned Parenthood clinic. She makes her way to the front desk, gives the clerk her name, and hands her some identification. The desk clerk checks her ID, enters her information into a computer, and hands her a clipboard with forms to fill out. Symoné takes a seat in the waiting area and starts to fill out the forms. A few moments pass, and her name is called over a loud speaker. "Symoné Harris! Symoné Harris!"

Symoné gets up, walks over to the clerk, and hands her the clipboard. The clerk presses a buzzer underneath her desk and directs Symoné to a side door. "You can go through that door to the lab. Fidencia Jorge will speak with you before your exam and afterwards," the desk clerk informs her.

❋   ❋   ❋

Symoné looks nervous as she walks into the counselor's office after her examination. She sits and scans the awareness posters on the walls about abstinence, date rape, domestic violence, drugs, crisis hotlines, and pro-choice.

The counselor, Fidencia, enters the office with Symoné's chart in her hand. "Hello again, Symoné. Examination went well?"

"Yes."

Fidencia takes a seat behind her desk, opens the chart, and goes over the doctor's notes. "So, how are you feeling?"

"I've been extremely tried. I haven't been able to sleep and I can't seem to hold any food down."

"Well, according to the doctor's exam and your test results, you're pregnant."

"What?"

"You're pregnant."

"Could there possibly be a mistake?"

"There's no mistake, sweetie. That's why we gave you the blood test to be sure."

"Do you know how many weeks?"

"You are almost twelve weeks."

The room falls silent. Symoné's eyes fill with tears. Fidencia hands her a tissue and comforts her.

"So what's your next available date for an abortion?"

"Are you sure? You do have options, like giving the baby up for adoption."

Symoné's mind drifts as Fidencia speaks. "You don't have to make this decision today. Go home and speak with your family." She hands Symoné her business card. "If you need to talk or have any questions, do not hesitate to give me a call, okay?"

Symoné takes Fidencia's business card, thanks her, and leaves.

❋ ❋ ❋

Symoné rushes through the double doors at Christ the King Regional High School and into the gymnasium toward the girls' locker room, holding her cheerleader bag and pom-poms in her hand. The basketball team is jogging out of the locker room onto the gym floor to warm up. When Mike sees Symoné he breaks the line to talk with her.

"Symoné, where have you been all day?"

"I was at the doctor's office."

"Is everything okay?" Mike asks, touching Symoné's stomach. "What's the matter, you pregnant or something?"

Symoné pushes his hand away.

The basketball coach comes out of the boys' locker room. "Mike, why aren't you warming up with the team? We have a game to win. Let's go!"

"Okay, coach. Symoné, we'll go get something to eat and talk after the game." Mike kisses Symoné and joins his teammates on the gym floor.

Symoné enters the girls' locker room. Some of the cheerleaders are practicing cheers and others are putting on uniforms. Her friend Chrissy is in uniform, pinning up her bun at the vanity mirror. She sees Symoné come into the locker room through the mirror. Chrissy notices her holding her stomach, the nauseated look on her face, and bags under her eyes.

Symoné walks over to her locker, opens it, and takes a seat on the bench. Chrissy walks over and sits on the bench next to Symoné.

"What's the matter? Girl, you look terrible," Chrissy says.

Symoné takes a deep breath, then looks at Chrissy. "I'm pregnant."

"You're what?"

"I'm pregnant," Symoné confirms, looking Chrissy in her eyes.

"How do you know?"

"I just came from the doctor's."

Chrissy continues to stare at Symoné with a shocked look on her face. "What are you going to do? Does Mike know yet?"

"No, I'm going to tell him after the game."

The cheerleading coach enters the locker room. She blows the whistle hanging on the lanyard around her neck, looks at her wristwatch, and starts clapping her hands together. "Ladies, let's go! I need you out on the gym floor in thirty seconds."

The cheerleaders rush out the locker room and the coach follows. Symoné hurries to put on her uniform, while Chrissy touches up her makeup in the mirror.

As Kharizma and GiGi exit the locker room, they walk by Symoné, making comments about Mike.

"Symoné, your man is looking real good on that court lately," Kharizma says.

"Yeah girl, you better watch him," GiGi warns, as she looks Symoné up and down.

"Before somebody try to scoop his ass up," Kharizma adds. She attempts to leave when Chrissy lunges on Kharizma, grabs her hair, and bangs her head into the locker. Kharizma is caught off guard and starts swinging wildly. Symoné quickly moves out the way as Kharizma falls over the bench and onto the locker room floor.

"FUCKING, TRIFLING BITCH!" Chrissy shrieks, as she punches and kicks Kharizma repeatedly. Kharizma tries to kick her back, swinging savagely to try and protect her face from the vicious blows Chrissy is landing. Symoné and GiGi try to tear the girls apart.

"Chrissy, stop before you get in trouble," Symoné yells. "She ain't worth it!"

"Fuck that, this BITCH talks too much!" Chrissy says, trying to get a few more punches in.

"Fuck you, too, hoe!" Kharizma responds, kicking Chrissy's stomach.

Symoné and GiGi finally separate the girls. Chrissy is out of breath as she walks over to the vanity mirror. She plops down into the chair and fixes her makeup, as Symoné tries to fix her friend's hair.

"Bitch fucked up my hair," Chrissy growls.

Symoné smiles and shakes her head. "Girl, you out of control."

"You let that bitch get away with too much shit," Chrissy says.

Kharzima is by the lockers. She takes a baby wipe from her locker and cleans her face, then brushes her smooth hair back into a ponytail, while GiGi wipes the dirt off her uniform.

The cheerleading coach comes back into the locker room, vexed. "What's going on, ladies? Why are we not on the floor yet?"

"Ask Kharizma," Chrissy responds with an attitude.

"What kind of example are you setting, Kharizma?" the coach demands looking in Kharizma's direction. "You're the captain. You're supposed to be out on the gym floor before the squad."

"You're right, coach," Kharizma agrees. Before she and GiGi exit the locker room, she rolls her eyes at Chrissy one more time. Symoné and Chrissy make their way out next, the cheerleading coach behind them.

❀   ❀   ❀

There is a private children's party going on at Sammy's in City Island. Symoné and Mike sit at a cozy table in a quiet corner. The waitress arrives with water for the table, takes their orders, and leaves.

"Good game today," Symoné says.

"It was all right. My jump shot was a little off. So how was your day?" Mike asks.

"Besides breaking up a fight in the locker room between Chrissy and Kharizma, okay I guess."

"Chrissy and Kharizma were fighting, really? About what?"

"About Kharizma running her mouth too much and being disrespectful."

The waitress arrives with their food and drinks.

"Damn, that's crazy. But forget about that. What happened at the doctor's office today?"

"Can we talk about that after we eat?"

"Now you got me worried. What's going on, Symoné?"

"I'm pregnant, Mike."

"We're having a baby?"

"Yeah," she says. She puts her head down and begins to cry. "I need to tell you something, Mike."

"Symoné, what's the matter? You don't want to have my baby?"

"No, Mike, that's not it. Of course I would love to have your baby. It's just . . . I am looking forward to attending Spelman in August . . . and, I know you looking forward to playing ball with USC."

Mike moves his chair closer to Symoné and takes her hand. "I got you."

"We are going to be all right. Don't worry."

Symoné tries to crack a smile.

Mike flags the waitress over, begins to eat and talk about his plans for the expected baby; he does not realize Symoné is no longer listening.

Her focus is on the little girl's birthday celebration across the restaurant. The hostess brings a cake to the table with lit candles. The other waitresses and waiters gather around the little girl and everyone sings Happy Birthday. Symoné begins to fiddle with the heart-shaped locket and drifts off into deep thoughts of a happier time in her childhood; her kindergarten graduation, with her hair full of Shirley Temple curls, the pretty, fluffy, lavender dress she wore, and the matching lavender patent leather shoes. That day Symoné's dad surprised her with a very special graduation gift, a beautiful, shiny 18-carat gold, heart-shaped locket. Inside was Symoné's favorite picture and an inscription that read:

I am always with you. I am your knight in shining armor, here to protect you and keep you safe, now and always, Love Daddy.

A tear falls from her eyes.

"You okay?" Mike interrupts.

Symoné snaps out of her daydream, with a faint smile on her face.

"Yeah, I'm just thinking about my dad."

"Symoné, what do you think your dad would say to us getting married?"

"Married?"

"Yeah, why not?"

"What about college, Mike?"

"Come with me to USC. We'll get a place off campus."

"Would you have asked me to get married if I wasn't pregnant?"

"It's the right thing to do."

❄ ❄ ❄

It's the end of the night. Symoné and Mike sit in his jeep parked in front of her house.

"Symoné, I'm serious about getting married. I love you and I want us to be a family."

"I don't know, Mike," she said. The tears fall from her eyes, as she stares into Mike's.

He takes his championship ring, grabs her left hand, and attempts to put the oversized ring on her finger. She pulls her hand away.

"I can't, Mike. I need to tell you something."

"I don't want an answer now," Mike interrupts. "Just think about it, that's all I ask." He kisses Symoné gently and they say goodnight.

Symoné exits the Jeep with her bags and hurries to the front door. Mike sits and watches her to make sure she is safe in the house.

Symoné digs through her bags, searching for her house keys. She is feeling nauseous and starts to gag. Overwhelmed, she puts a hand over her mouth and bangs on the door with the other. The door opens. It is Fisher, dressed in gray sweat pants and a t-shirt with a police logo on the upper left side. He finds her bent over, holding her stomach. She pushes the door open, drops her bags at the door, rushing into the house, almost knocking Fisher over. Fisher, with the door still open, waves bye to Mike, and closes it. Mike pulls off down the street.

Fisher sits back down on the sofa and continues to read the Amsterdam News. He hears what sounds like Symoné gagging and vomiting in the guest bathroom. He stops reading, gets up, and investigates. He opens the door and finds Symoné with her jacket on. She's down on her knees, with her face in the toilet, throwing up.

Symoné empties all she can out of her stomach. She takes tissue, wipes her mouth, and pulls herself up from the floor by holding onto the sink. Symoné is once again face-to-face with that image of her reflection in the mirror, covered in dirt, frail, and worn down.

Fisher stands in the bathroom doorway, watching Symoné. She sees him through the mirror, but pretends not to see him and turns on the water to wash her hands.

"What's wrong with you?" Fisher asks.

Symoné turns and angrily looks Fisher in the face. "I'm pregnant, Jack."

"Who's the father?"

Symoné doesn't answer and walks out the bathroom.

❋ ❋ ❋

Moonlight fills the dark room. Symoné is in her bed crying. She hears the knob turning on her bedroom door and holds her breath. Her bedroom door opens and Fisher's silhouette appears in the doorway. His monstrous shadow is reflected off the bedroom wall. She lies very still and slowly reaches for the kitchen knife under her pillow. He walks toward the bed, stops suddenly, and leaves her bedroom, closing the door behind him. She takes a deep breath, with the knife still in her hand, turns over on her back, and stares up into the darkness at the ceiling, as tears fall down her face.

A MOTHER'S LOVE

· ·

CHAPTER 6

A weary Mae, still dressed in her nurse's uniform, walks into the house, carrying her purse and the mail. After hanging her coat, she sits on the sofa, places the mail on the coffee table, takes her shoes off, and begins to massage a foot.

Fisher comes into the living room, wearing his bulletproof vest and 9mm holstered on his side. He walks over to the sofa and sits next to Mae.

"Long night, huh?" Fisher asks, as he initiates massaging her feet.

"Yeah. Oh, that feels good," Mae says, leaning back. She relaxes into the massage and begins to describe her day. "I worked the trauma unit tonight. It was crazy; five gunshot victims - all teens, three child abuse cases - children under ten, two battered and one sexually assaulted. My God, what's the world coming to?"

"What you need is a vacation."

"I wish I could, but the hospital needs me."

"Believe you me, the hospital will survive without you," Fisher responds, as he starts to massage her tense shoulders. "Mae, that hospital's been your entire life since Vaughan died."

"Yes, I know."

"You need to start living your life again."

"What life? He was my life."

"Mae, I'm single, you're alone . . . Let's get married."

"Fisher, you and me get married? Please, stop joking around."

"All right, I may be moving too fast about us getting married, but I'm serious about us being together, Mae. How long have we known each other, now?" Fisher asks.

Mae looks at him in the eyes, "A long time Jack -since high school."

"Yeah, you were my girl before Vaughan stole you away."

"No. He didn't steal me – you had too many women and were a bit of a player back in the day."

"Okay, okay, you got that one, but Vaughan is gone, Mae, and he's not coming back."

"Fisher, I, I don't know. I have Symoné to consider. What is she going to think?" Mae stammers.

Fisher's beeper goes off. He takes it from his waist and looks at the display. "Mae, I have to go. I'm meeting some of the fellas over at the sports bar to watch the game." He grabs his jacket from the coat closet and hurries out the door.

Mae gets up from the couch and walks into the kitchen. She peeks through the window curtain, a smile on her face as Fisher pulls off.

❋ ❋ ❋

The next evening Mae is cooking dinner when the front door opens. Symoné enters, carrying her cheerleading bag and Louis Vuitton backpack, and is surprised to see her mother home so early. She hangs her bags on the coat rack and goes into the kitchen.

"You're home? What a surprise," Symoné says and kisses her mother on the cheek. She grabs a soda from the refrigerator, sits on a stool at the kitchen bar, and starts her homework.

"I asked for the night off," Mae says.

Symoné inhales. "It smells good in here. What are you cooking?"

"Roast beef, beans and rice, cabbage with smoked turkey wings, pineapple cornbread, and your favorite, coconut cake."

"It must be a very special occasion, because you haven't cooked like this or taken a night off since daddy passed."

"I know," Mae replies, sitting next to her daughter. "Symoné, we need to talk about something important."

Symoné stops working on her homework. "Mommy, you aren't sick or something?"

"No, I'm okay. I'm not sick."

"What's going on, then?" Symoné puts her pen down and turns to her mother.

"What do you think about Jack?" Mae asks seriously.

Symoné lowers her eyes. Her face becomes tense as she looks at Mae from the corner of her eyes. "Why?"

"Well, I haven't been out with anyone or dated since your daddy died, and I've been very lonely," Mae explains, gently touching Symoné's hand.

Symoné looks at her mother. "You're ready to start dating?"

"I think so. Jack ask me . . ."

"Jack?" Symoné looks bewildered. "What about him?"

"What you think about him making this his permanent residence?"

"What?" Symoné exclaims, pulling her hand back. Symoné gets up off the stool and looks at Mae with utter disgust. "You can't be serious."

"We're just talking, Symoné. I just wanted to know your thoughts."

"My thoughts? There is none. I can't understand why he is still here. My daddy died months ago. What do you think the neighbors and the officers at daddy's precinct are whispering about, behind closed doors knowing Jack's being here so long?"

"Excuse me?" Mae snaps.

"My daddy's probably rolling over in his grave right now, to think that you would even consider getting with . . ." Mae slaps Symoné across the face.

"How dare you talk to me like that? What has Jack ever done to you?"

"Everything," Symoné responds angrily.

"Everything, like what, Symoné?" Mae asks.

"He touched me, that's what."

"Touched you? What do you mean by he touched you?"

"What do you think I mean?"

"What? Girl, you going crazy, Jack would never. Why would you be so hateful and tell such a lie."

"You think I would make that up?"

"I don't know. I know you love your father very much."

"Yes, I do, and right now I wish he was here." She storms out the house, slamming the door behind her.

Mae rushes over to the door and opens it, but Symoné is gone. Mae is concerned, as she stands quietly at the doorway. She inhales and then quietly shuts the door.

❋ ❋ ❋

Symoné walks along the promenade at the Riverbank State Park in Harlem. Depressed and in a daze, she notices a little girl holding her mother's hand, as they walk a Shih Tzu with a rhinestone collar. A man jogs in the opposite direction with earphones on.

The dog gets away from the small child, and she takes off running after her pet. Her mother, not too far behind, calls the dog by name. "Scarlett, come here, girl," she says over and over again.

The jogging man sees the Shih Tzu heading his way and the little girl chasing it. He jogs a little faster to try and head the dog off. The Shih Tzu runs by Symoné and its chain tangles around Symoné's feet, almost causing her to fall. She tries to untangle the chain, but the Shih Tzu is jumping up and down, playing, licking, and nibbling at her hands. The jogging man stops and helps Symoné by petting the dog to calm her down, and manages to untangle the chain. Once the Shih Tzu is free, the man picks it up, and it starts licking his face.

"I think she likes you," Symoné says.

"Yeah, I think so. Hi, I'm Craig Little."

Craig Little holds out his hand and they shake.

"My name is Symoné," she responds with a smile.

The little girl and her mother run up to Symoné and Craig Little. The mother is very apologetic. "Forgive me, please, I am so sorry," the woman says.

"Don't worry about it," Symoné responds.

Craig Little hands the dog back to the little girl and her mother. The mother puts the Shih Tzu back down on the ground, scolds the little girl, and hands her back the leash as they continue down the promenade. Symoné watches with a smile on her face, as the little girl skips with her dog.

"So, what you doing out here, walking by yourself?" Craig Little asks.

"Why? And who's asking?" Symoné replies.

Craig Little's pager beeps. He takes it off his waist and looks at the number. Symoné attempts to walk off.

"Where you off to so fast?"

"Who wants to know?"

Craig Little's pager continuously beeps. He ignores it.

"Damn baby, I'm just trying to be friendly."

"Why? By the way, your beeper is going off; don't sound like you need a friend."

"Just a little business that needs my attention, but it can wait." Craig Little turns off his pager.

"Can I get a number, so we can continue this conversation another time? Maybe over dinner?"

"I have a lot going on right now."

"Take my number at least, and when you don't have a lot going on, give me a call."

Craig Little takes a pen and piece of paper out of his pocket, writes his number, and hands it to Symoné.

"I'll be waiting for that call, Symoné," Craig Little says and jogs off.

✳ ✳ ✳

Mike is watching a basketball game on TV when the doorbell rings. He answers and is happy to find Symoné standing in the doorway. She comes in and sits on the sofa. Mikes sits next to her.

"Where you been? Your mother's been blowing-up my beeper all night."

"Walking," she says.

"Are you hungry? Want something to eat or drink?" he asks.

"Not really."

Mike goes into the kitchen to get them something to drink.

"Where's Eddie, away again?" she asks, picking up an old picture of Mike, Eddie, and their mother in Disney World.

"Every time I come here and look at this picture, it makes me smile. Ya'll look so cute."

Mike comes into the living room, carrying two bottles of Tropicana orange juice. "Just in case you get thirsty," he says, putting the bottles down on the coffee table.

"Your mother was beautiful."

"Yeah, she was."

Symoné puts the picture down, lies across Mike's lap, and flips through the channels with the remote. Mike takes the remote and changes it back to the SportsChannel. "So, what's going on, Symoné?"

"My mother and I had a big fight."

"You told her about the baby?"

"Not yet. We got into it about Jack."

"Your Godfather?"

"Yeah."

"What happen?"

"I tried to tell her something and she didn't want to believe me, my own mother."

"About Jack?"

"Yea, about Jack."

"What about him?"

"I don't want to talk about it. I just want out of that house," she snaps, sitting up from Mike's lap.

"I hear you loud and clear. But right now you need to call you mother."

"I really don't feel like talking to her right now."

Mike hands Symoné the phone. "At least let her know that you are okay."

"Mike, can I trust you?"

"Of course you can."

"Do you think I would ever lie to you?"

"No, why would you."

"And, will you always love me no matter what?"

Mike looks into Symoné's eyes. "Forever, no matter what," he promises and kisses her on the forehead. Symoné gives Mike a hug and calls her mother, while he continues watching the basketball game.

❋   ❋   ❋

Fisher sits behind the conference table at Internal Affairs, leaning back in a swivel chair, chewing on the inside of his bottom lip. His open folder and a mini tape recorder are before him, as Investigators Washington and Jones continue their interview about the night his partner, Detective Vaughn Harris, was murdered.

"It is also my duty to inform you that you are obligated to answer questions and provide full and complete information to Investigator Jones and myself. Less than complete candor during any statement may lead to serious disciplinary sanctions, which may include suspension or termination. Do you understand what I have just stated, Detective Jack Fisher?" Investigator Washington asks.

"Yes, I understand. Just want to know if I am under investigation, and whether this investigation could lead to any form of discipline, punitive, or adverse action against me," Fisher responds.

"Are you concerned?" Washington asks.

"No, not at all," Fisher lies, leaning back, comfortable and confident.

Investigator Jones jumps into questioning, hoping to ease the tension between Fisher and Washington. "The answer to your question is no," Jones says. "Because you are being administratively ordered to answer questions, nothing you say may be used in a subsequent criminal proceeding. Now, can we proceed?" Jones concludes, as he picks up his pen and starts to write on a yellow pad.

"Yes," Fisher says.

"My name is Detective Jack Fisher, badge #66666, hired January 3, 1978. My present assignment is desk duty. My assignment on the day in question was an undercover operation, in pursuit of a notorious drug gang, which is run by Craig Little out of the Dunbar Housing Complex in Harlem, between 149th and 150th Street."

"Detective Fisher, please tell me what occurred on Tuesday, September 8," Washington requests.

"I was detaining a drug suspect when another man approached us. Detective Vaughan Harris drew his gun, told me to watch out, and shot his gun, killing the suspect, Coolridge Charles a.k.a. Caz. In all the chaos, the suspect I was detaining got away," Fisher explains.

"So you didn't put handcuffs on the suspect while you were detaining him? What about the suspect's name? And wasn't there a third suspect?" Washington asks.

"There was a third, but I was only able to catch one. The other got away," Fisher says.

"No, actually two suspects got away, one suspect is dead, and not mention your partner," Washington says.

"So you saying I didn't do my job and caused my partner's death?"

Jones stops writing and intervenes. "Of course that's not what we're saying."

The pager beeping on his side distracts Fisher. He looks at the number on the display; it's Mae. "I did my job and I followed proper protocol." His pager starts beeping again.

"Do you need to take a break to answer your pager?" Jones asks.

"Thank you," Fisher says, and picks up the telephone in the conference room to call Mae.

Jones stops writing and turns off the tape recorder. He and Washington try to eavesdrop.

"Hello Mae. Is everything okay?" Fisher asks, and nods his head as she responds. "I'm sure Symoné's all right and probably at a girlfriend's house. I will talk to you when I get out of my meeting. Stop worrying, okay?" Then he hangs up.

"Is everything okay? Do we need to reschedule?" Jones asks.

"Something I need to handle, but it can wait. I want to get this interview over with," Fisher replies.

Jones turns on the recorder, and Washington continues his questioning.

"So, according to your recollection of the incident on Tuesday, September 8, the dead suspect, Coolridge Charles a.k.a Caz, came up behind you and shot your partner, Detective Vaughan Harris, in the head? Your partner was able to pull off one shot before getting hit, killing the suspect instantly with one shot through the heart?" Washington inquires.

"That's correct," Fisher confirms.

Washington hands Fisher a yellow pad and pen. "Could you map out the scene for us, step by step, around the time when the shooting started?"

"It's right here in my incident report," Fisher says, pushing his report toward the investigators. "You should also have a copy in your investigation file."

Washington looks over the report and hands it to Jones, who glances at the report and hands it back to Fisher.

"We have an eyewitness that says differently," Jones remarks.

"Eyewitness?" Fisher responds and sits up in his chair. "Who? One of NYPD's paid informants?" He starts to chew his inner lip.

"We received an anonymous tip that claims you tried to rob the drug dealer that escaped and planted the gun on the dead suspect," Washington explains.

"What are you saying? You believe the informant?"

"No, we're just trying to find out the truth about what happened the night of September 8," Jones explains.

"I will, of course, answer all of your questions, but at this point in time, I request to have a representative assist me prior to answering any more questions. I'm entitled to that," Fisher states.

"If you have nothing further to say, Detective Fisher, this interview is over. Time is eleven p.m., on Friday, June 9, 1989," Washington says before turning off the tape recorder.

Fisher also turns off his tape recorder and puts it in his shirt pocket. He picks up his folder off the table and leaves the conference room.

Washington bangs his fist on the table. "He's fucking dirty. I can smell it, a real fucking Judas. I know he had something to do with Detective Harris's murder."

"Don't sweat it, Washington. It's just a matter of time, just a matter of time before the walls start caving in on his ass," Jones says.

❋ ❋ ❋

The moonlight is shining through the blinds in Mike's bedroom. Basketball posters and newspaper clippings of Mike's basketball accomplishments hang on the walls. Large trophies are in every corner of the room and dresser.

Symoné is asleep and breathing heavily. Sweat is glistening on her forehead as she mumbles through a nightmare. She opens her eyes suddenly, holding her stomach. She turns and looks over at the clock. It reads one a.m. She picks up the framed picture of her and Mike next to the clock. Tears fall from her eyes. She wipes them away, placing the picture back down. She sits up on the edge of the bed and begins putting on her shoes. She lifts her head and finds herself staring into the mirror attached to the dresser in front of Mike's bed. As she begins to fix her hair Symoné, once again, sees that dreadful reflection of herself.

Mike quietly walks over to Symoné. He turns her around, stares into her eyes, and wipes the tears from her face. The image in the mirror of the dirty, frail, worn down, young woman disappears.

"What's the matter, Symoné?"

Symoné puts her head down, too ashamed to look Mike in the face.

"It's . . ."

"What? You're still thinking about your mother and Jack?"

She nods yes.

"Symoné, let's get our own place."

"What?"

"You can move in with my brother and me until we find our own."

"I don't know, Mike. Everything is just so crazy right now."

"You don't have to give me an answer right now. It's late and you had a rough day. Why don't you lie back down and try to get some more rest. I will take you home in the morning."

Mike kisses Symoné on the forehead, takes her by the hand, and they lie on the bed together. He wraps his arm around her and pulls her close until they fall asleep.

❊ ❊ ❊

It is the next morning. Fisher is in the living room, comforting Mae while she drinks her coffee. Mae has bags under her eyes and looks exhausted. The front door opens and in comes Symoné and Mike. Mae jumps up from the couch, rushing over to the door and gives Symoné a tight hug.

"Symoné, I was worried sick about you. I thought you were coming home last night," Mae says.

"Sorry. I fell asleep at Mike's."

Mae puts her arm around Symoné's shoulders as they walk toward the couch. Mike follows quietly. Fisher moves over to make room for Mae and Symoné. Symoné sits on the love seat with Mike, across from Mae and Fisher on the sofa.

"Symoné, I was worried sick."

"I meant to call you back. I was tired and needed a nap. I didn't think I was going to go to sleep so long."

"You've been doing a lot of sleeping lately and been very moody. What's going on?"

Symoné looks at Fisher. She shrugs her shoulders and then puts her head down. Mike looks at Fisher suspiciously.

"I'm moving out."

"Yes, I know in a few months you'll be at Spelman."

"No, I won't. I'll be at USC, off-campus with Mike."

"What?"

"I, I'm," Symoné stammers.

Mike puts his arm around Symoné.

"I'm pregnant."

"You're what?" Mae grabs ahold of Fisher's hand.

"I'm having a baby."

"Symoné, what were you thinking? What's going on with you lately? Since your father died you have changed. I'm very worried about you."

You think Mike and I planned this or wanted it to happen? YOU REALLY THINK I WANT THIS BABY?"

Mike stares at Symoné in shock and disbelief to learn that she doesn't want the baby.

"Okay now, everybody relax," Fisher interjects.

Mae lets go of Fisher's hand. She gets up from the sofa and points her finger at Symoné. "Well, you and Mike sure didn't take the necessary precautions to try and prevent this situation from happening."

Fisher is sweating now and starts chewing on the inside of his bottom lip. Symoné gets up from the love seat. Mike tries to pull her back down, but she pulls away from him.

"Mike and I? Really, are you working that hard, and that tired, that you can't even see what's really going on around you?"

"See what?" Mae responds rapidly. "I see you got yourself pregnant and throwing your life away."

"You just don't get it, mom, and you never will." Symoné storms out the living room and up the stairs to her bedroom.

"Excuse me, Mrs. Harris. I'll go talk with her." Mike follows Symoné up the stairs.

Fisher takes a deep breath and leans his head back on the sofa. Mae plops down on the sofa, agitated and upset. Fisher sits up and starts massaging her shoulders.

"I'm going to set-up an appointment for her to see a therapist first thing in the morning. I should have done this a long time ago."

"Counseling would be good for her," Fisher says.

A FOOL IN LOVE

· ·

CHAPTER 7

End of the summer, August 1989.

It's Mike's last summer tournament before he heads off to USC. He is playing in the championship game at the West Fourth Street Courts, also known as "The Cage," in New York City's Greenwich Village, where notable players like Julius Winfield Erving II, commonly known by the nickname Dr. J played. A pregnant Symoné is courtside, watching the game with Chrissy, Georgie, Eddie, and Hershey.

The fourth quarter is about to end. The score is even. Mike leaps high off the ground, grabs a rebound with his long arms, and takes the ball all the way down the court, faking out the other players with his fancy moves. They are tripping and falling over each other. He jumps over the other team's player, spread eagle over the player's head, and dunks the basketball. The crowd is standing and going wild, yelling, "MIKE NICE, MIKE NICE!"

The DJ plays Kurtis Blow's, "Basketball". The chorus "We're playing basketball, we love that basketball" repeats itself and blasts through the large speakers surrounding the park. Georgie and Mike's teammates rush over to the champ, smothering him with hugs and high-fives.

Kharizma and GiGi are at the game. Kharizma runs onto the court and throws herself on Mike. He is caught off guard when she hugs and kisses him on the mouth. Mike is also swept up in the moment. He hugs Kharizma back, lifting her off the ground, and then puts her back down. Mike is talking and laughing with Kharizma and GiGi. Symoné and Chrissy look at each other in disbelief. Symoné is furious.

"What part of the game is that?" she exclaims to Chrissy, then gets up off the bleachers and attempts to walk over to Mike, but is stopped by Eddie.

"Symoné, don't sweat that. It's nothing. Let's meet Mike back at the car and go out to celebrate," Eddie says.

Mike sees Eddie talking with a very pissed off Symoné.

"Nah, that's okay, I'm not hungry. Tell your brother I'll see him at the house, I'm out," Symoné retorts and walks off with Chrissy.

Mike cuts his conversation short with Kharizma, breaks away from the crowd, and hurries over to Symoné, but it is too late. She has left the park.

❊   ❊   ❊

Symoné and Mike's live together in a cozy one-bedroom apartment on Strivers Row in Harlem. It's passed midnight and Symoné is home alone in the bed, reading an *Essence* magazine. She hears the front door of the apartment open and close. She looks over at the clock; it reads 12:59 AM. Mike walks into the bedroom, carrying a take-out bag from Jackson Hole Burgers. Soaking wet from the rain, walks over to Symoné, takes the magazine, and tries to give her a kiss. She turns her face away. He hands the take-out bag to Symoné, then takes off his jacket and hat, and hangs it on the door. Symoné opens the bag, pulls out a cheeseburger platter, and begins to eat. She spits the food out.

"Why would you bring me this cold ass food, Mike?" Symoné asks as she slams the bag down on the nightstand. "I'm sure Kharimza's man don't bring her home cold food."

"Come on now, why you acting like that?"

"Ask that fake ass bitch, Kharizma."

"Kharizma? Come on, Symoné, I know you're not serious."

"How can you let her disrespect me like that?"

"Like what? It was a game and a friend came over to congratulate me and wish me luck at USC this season."

"So now you're going to play stupid? You know that bitch knew I was there. She want you and tryin' to make me jealous, and you fed into the bullshit."

"I don't care about that girl. I'm with you, you're carrying my baby, and I thought we'd be hanging out after the game, but you were M.I.A."

"Yeah, um hum."

"Come on, Symoné. I'm not going through this with you tonight."

"Yeah, you will go through it."

Mike grabs his basketball in the corner of the bedroom and leaves. Symoné get out of bed to follow Mike, but has a sharp excruciating pain and falls back onto the bed bent over holding her stomach.

❋ ❋ ❋

It's dark outside. The Rucker's basketball court is empty, half lit, and wet from the rain. Mike walks onto the court with his basketball tucked under his arm. He takes off his jacket, throwing it on the wet bench and starts shooting, letting his frustrations out on the court. He works up a sweat, running up and down the court, shooting baskets from all angles, dunking and pretending there are other players on the court. He suddenly stops playing and is exhausted. He puts the basketball on the ground and wipes the sweat from his face with the front of his t-shirt. Mike hears his pager going off. It's Symoné. He grabs his jacket and hurries to his jeep.

❋ ❋ ❋

Mike enters the bedroom and sees Symoné on the side of the bed, bent over and moaning. He hurries over and helps her up onto the bed.

"I'm sorry, Mike."

"Symoné, it's okay, don't worry about that. Let's get you to the hospital. Did you call your mother?"

"No," she says and lies back on the bed, clutching her stomach. Symoné's eyes start to fill with tears, as she watches Mike gather her things.

Mike picks up the telephone and calls Mae.

"Hello? Mrs. Harris? We're on our way to Harlem Hospital. Something's wrong with Symoné. I think she's losing the baby. I'll see you at the hospital." Mike hangs up the cordless phone. He takes Symoné's coat out of the closet, helps her put it on, and they make their way out the door.

❄ ❄ ❄

Mike and Symoné enter Harlem Hospital. Symoné is having a difficult time walking. Mike is sweating and nervous as he helps her through the revolving doors.

Mae and Fisher are already at the hospital. Mae is at the entrance with a wheelchair. Fisher attempts to help Mike put Symoné into the wheelchair. Symoné pulls away from Fisher and holds tightly to Mike. Mike looks bewildered, switching his gaze between Fisher and Symoné.

Dr. Kay Ramsey and a team of nurses are waiting to receive Symoné at the maternity ward. The elevator doors open. Mae exits with Symoné and hands the wheelchair off to the nurse.

"Hello Mae, Mike," Dr. Ramsey says. "How are you feeling, Symoné?"

"Not good. The sharp pain is coming back to back," Symoné moans.

"It's a little soon for the baby to be coming. Have you been under any type of stress lately?"

"Not really."

"Mae, you guys go relax in the waiting area. I'm going to examine Symoné and make sure the baby is okay."

"Is it all right if Mike comes, Dr. Ramsey?" Symoné asks.

"Yes, of course."

Mae and Fisher watch as the nurse rolls Symoné down the corridor. Mike follows them and carries Symoné's bag. Mike turns to glance at Fisher oddly, then hurries down the corridor. Dr. Ramsey is asking Symoné questions, as a nurse writes the responses on a clipboard. Symoné is in too much pain to answer any more questions, so Mike answers for her.

❄ ❄ ❄

Moments later, they enter the delivery room. Dr. Ramsey walks over to the sink and scrubs her arms and hands. A delivery nurse is helping Mike put on his scrubs. The OB tech is setting up a table of instruments to be used during the delivery. The anesthesiologist is preparing medications. A neonatologist is also on hand in case the baby is at risk. If Dr. Ramsey must perform a cesarean, an incubator is already in the corner of the delivery room.

Symoné is on the birthing bed, her heels in the stirrups. An electronic fetal monitor is attached to her abdomen to keep track of the baby. Mike gently dabs the sweat on Symoné's face and brow with a damp cloth, as she focuses on breathing like she learned in Lamaze class. Tears are falling from her eyes as she digs her nails into Mike's arm.

Dr. Ramsey examines Symoné. "Yes, the baby is definitely coming. I need you to try not to push."

"It hurts," Symoné moans. She tries to sit up; two nurses hold her down and try to keep her legs apart, while Dr. Ramsey tries to conduct the exam.

"Symoné, you have to relax before you hurt yourself and the baby," Mike says. "Did someone let her mother know that she is in labor?"

"Yes, the nurse informed her," Dr. Ramsey says.

Symoné's contractions are now coming faster, causing her to scream.

"Doc, is there anything you can give her for the pain?" Mike asks.

"Symoné, would you like something to ease the pain?" Dr. Ramsey inquires.

Symoné nods her head yes.

"Okay, I'm going to let the anesthesiologist give you the epidural to alleviate some of the pain. Hopefully in a little while you will be fully dilated, and we can deliver the baby. I'll be right back," Dr. Ramsey explains.

"I need you to turn on your side and move to the edge of the bed," the anesthesiologist directs.

Symoné turns to her side and grabs hold of Mike's hand. The anesthesiologist cleans her back and injects the area with numbing medicine. Symoné squeezes Mike's hand tighter and closes her eyes.

"First, I am going to give you a small dose, followed by a full dose, provided there are no problems. You will start to feel numb in about ten to twenty minutes. I will monitor the baby's heart rate and your blood pressure to make sure both of you aren't having any negative effects from the medicine, okay?"

Symoné nods her head. Mike is very attentive to Symoné and does all he can to keep her calm and relaxed.

❋ ❋ ❋

Thirty minutes later, the medication hasn't kicked in and the labor room nurse calls for Dr. Ramsey. Dr. Ramsey hurries to the labor room.

"The monitor shows the baby's heart rate is dropping between contractions," the nurse whispers to Dr. Ramsey.

Dr. Ramsey sits on the stool, lifting the sheet covering Symoné. "Symoné, you are fully dilated and the baby is coming. Take a deep breath and give me one big push."

Symoné leans forward, lets out one big scream, and with all her might, she pushes.

"I need you to push again," Dr. Ramsey says.

"No, I can't. It hurts," Symoné exclaims.

"Come on, Symoné, you can do it," Mike assures.

"Doc, her pressure is dropping," the nurse reveals.

"I can't. I don't want it," Symoné screams. She is becoming incoherent and delirious. She looks up at Mike and sees Jack's face, then passes out.

Symoné regains consciousness and is swinging wildly. Mike and the nurses try to hold her arms down. She grabs onto Mike's arm and tries to sit up on the table. She is in and out of consciousness and mumbling into Mike's ear. "I tried to stop him, Mike."

"Stop who?"

"Jack."

"Jack . . . What about Jack?" Mike looks bewildered. He lets go of Symoné's hand and takes a step back, confused.

Dr. Ramsey looks over at the monitor with concern. "We're losing them. We have to take the baby."

Mike shifts his focus back to Symoné.

Symoné passes out again. She hears everything in the room, but is unable to move or speak. She is having an out-of-body experience.

❋   ❋   ❋

Symoné sees a tunnel with a bright, white light. Her body floats in the opposite direction, toward the darkness. She finds the image of the dirty, frail, and worn down, troubled, young woman that haunts her in the mirror. She's pregnant on a broken-down birthing table. Symoné looks around the room, disoriented and afraid.

Her mother, Mae, is dressed in all white, with a veil over her face, and there's a service dog on a leash. She is crying, being comforted by a man dressed in a doctor's uniform with a mask on. The man is peering from behind the mask. His eyes are dark and evil. The doctor pulls off the mask, and it is Jack Fisher. Symoné is terrified. She yells out for Mae to run, but no sounds are coming from her mouth. Mae lifts her veil and her eyes and mouth are sewn shut. With a bloody scalpel in hand, Fisher walks toward Symoné. Symoné is frantic and searches for a way out of the tunnel. A friendly and familiar male voice can be heard in the distance.

❋ ❋ ❋

"Symoné, wake up. It's Mike."

❋ ❋ ❋

The voice guides Symoné out of danger, away from Fisher, and back into the white light.

❋ ❋ ❋

"Symoné, wake up. It's Mike. What's going on, doc?"

"Mike, we are going to have to do an emergency c-section, before we lose them both," Dr. Ramsey explains.

A nurse quickly escorts Mike out of the labor room.

❋ ❋ ❋

Mike stands outside the neonatal intensive care unit, looking through a big glass window as nurses work on Symoné's baby. His hands and head are against the window. His eyes fill with tears. The baby's small body is hooked up to an IV and several machines.

Dr. Ramsey approaches. "Mike, your daughter will be fine. She has the best doctors and nurses and will receive the best care our hospital has to offer."

"That's good to hear," Mike says.

"Have you guys decided on a name?" Dr. Ramsey asks.

"Mykia Lorendale Harris," Mike whispers.

"Mykia, that's a beautiful name."

"Thanks." He is feeling melancholy and is still looking through the window. "So how's Symoné doing?" he asks.

"I would like Symoné to stay in the hospital a few more days. I want to make sure her pressure remains stable and run a few tests, just to make sure everything is okay. She gave us quite a scare in there."

"Yes, she did."

Dr. Ramsey walks away. Mae and Fisher walk up to the window to join Mike. Mae hugs Mike.

"She's so small and precious, Mike," Mae says.

Mike holds back his tears and smiles.

"It's going to be okay," Mae assures. "Don't worry."

Mike looks through the window with sadness in his eyes.

Fisher grabs Mike by the shoulders. "Congratulations, son."

Mike's face transforms. It is filled with hatred. His body becomes tense. Mike turns his head slightly down, looking at Fisher's hand on his shoulder. "Yeah … Thanks."

Fisher senses the tension in Mike's voice and removes his hand, backing away.

IT'S A NEW DAY

. . . .

CHAPTER 8

November 1989

It's a few months after Mykia's birth. Mike is home from USC for the Thanksgiving holiday break. Symoné is continuously picking arguments with Mike.

"Mike, why is it taking so long for you to find an apartment for us near campus. I'm starting to feel like you don't want us there."

"I have a lot on my plate right now with school and the team. It's been hard trying to find a place."

"You sure it's not because you met someone else at school?"

"Why every time I come home to visit it's a problem? Symoné, I'm trying to make this relationship work, but you keep pushing me away, accusing me of things I'm not doing, and saying craziness out your mouth. I know there is more going on. Just talk to me."

"I don't like this arrangement."

"Arrangement?"

"Yes, you off at USC and I'm here with the baby by myself."

"What are you saying, Symoné?"

"If we can't be together all the time, I'd rather not be together at all."

"Are you serious right now?"

Symoné goes to the closet, pulls out a suitcase, and puts it on the bed. "It's over, Mike. I want you to leave."

Mike is quiet. He starts pulling clothes out of the dresser and closet. He slowly folds the clothes and puts them into the suitcase. Symoné is sitting on the edge of the bed with tears in her eyes, watching Mike pack his things. He stops and tries to console her, but she pushes him away.

"Symoné, is this really what you want?"

Symoné nods her head yes. Mike closes the suitcase, then walks over to the crib and picks up Mykia giving her a hug and kiss. Then he pulls out some money and puts it on the nightstand.

"I'll be here if and when you want to talk, but not forever." Mike takes the suitcase off the bed then leaves.

The sound of the front door slamming wakes Mykia up and she starts to cry. Symoné takes Mykia out of the crib and comforts her. She walks over to the window, carrying Mykia and watches Mike get into his Jeep. Tears roll down her face uncontrollably as she watches Mike drive down the block.

❉ ❉ ❉

The next day the doorbell rings. Symoné hurries into the living room to answer the door. She swings the door open and finds her mother, Mae, holding a hand full of Kid's Gap shopping bags. Symoné is happy to see her mother, yet disappointed that it is not Mike.

"Hey Mom, how's it going?"

Mae comes in, puts down the bags, and sits on the sofa. "Where's my grandbaby?"

"Asleep in the room."

"What's the matter? You look like you've been crying. Where's Mike?"

"It's over between us."

"Over? What happened?"

"I just need some time."

"Time? Raising a baby alone is not easy. You may want to call Dr. Ramsey; you could be going through Postpartum. Some women get very depressed after they have a baby."

"Nah, it's not that. I have things to figure out and need the space and time to do it."

"You have anything in that fridge to eat? All this shopping got me hungry."

"There's some leftover spaghetti and meatballs." Symoné goes in the kitchen and heats up the leftovers.

"Mike's a fine young man and a good father, don't wait to long to call him and work things out."

Symoné reminiscences about the good times with Mike and her eyes start to water.

"Mom, I don't want to talk about Mike right now," she concludes, and walks over to the sofa, handing Mae her plate of food.

A car horn blows outside the living room window.

"Symoné! Hey Symoné," the voice outside the window yells.

The car horn blows repeatedly.

Symoné rushes over to the window and looks out. It's Chrissy in a white convertible GTI Volkswagen, with the music blaring through the brand new sound system. "You feel like going to the movies?"

Symoné pulls her head back inside. "Mom, could you watch Mykia, so I can catch a movie with Chrissy?"

"Go ahead and enjoy yourself," Mae says.

Symoné yells out the window, "I'm on my way down!"

"Thanks, Mom," she says, then heads for the door.

"SYMONÉ, you forgot something."

"What?"

"Aren't you going to say bye to Mykia?"

Symoné picks Mykia up out the playpen, gives her a kiss on the cheek, and leaves. "Mom, thanks for watching Mykia for me. I really need the break," she says, rushing out the door.

Symoné bolts down the stairs of the brownstone, when a 4Runner pulls up behind Chrissy's car and parks. Craig Little gets out of the 4Runner's passenger side, closes the door, and heads up the stairs to the brownstone. Symoné does not see Craig Little and bumps into him. She looks up and sees the guy she met in Riverside Park a few months ago.

"Craig Little?"

"Symoné, it has been a minute. How you been?"

"Good."

"I'm still waiting for that call. So when are you going to let me take you out or do you still have a lot going on?"

Symoné writes her number on a piece of paper and hands it to Craig Little. "I'm looking forward to your call," she says and continues down the stairs.

Craig Little watches Symoné with a smile on his face.

"I didn't know you knew Craig Little," Chrissy says.

"I don't. I met him when I was walking in Riverside Park a while back. What's his deal?"

"I hear he's one of the biggest drug dealers in Harlem, paid-in-full."

❅ ❅ ❅

The parking lot is crowded at the Whitestone Multiplex Cinemas, in the Bronx. Chrissy pulls into a parking space. She and Symoné get out and go into the movie theater. The ticket lines are long. The security guards are trying to keep the crowd orderly.

"Damn, look at the lines," Chrissy complains. "You feel like waiting?"

"Whatever."

They wait on the long line. Symoné is quiet and in a gloomy mood.

"Thinking about Mike?"

"Yeah, I miss him."

"Have you talked to him since last night?"

"Nah."

"I can't believe you put him out?"

"The distance between us, is taking its toll on me."

"Mykia needs her daddy in her life."

"I came out to have a good time, and I don't want to talk about Mike."

"So you're going to make it easy for the next chick? Mike's a fine ass man, on a basketball scholarship at USC, and no doubt getting drafted to the NBA, and you goin' let all that walk away?"

"Yeah, I just want to focus on me right now and raising Mykia."

"Symoné, don't turn around now, but there's this guy that keeps looking over here. He's the one wearing a White Sox's hat and an eight ball jacket."

Symoné waves at the guy and he waves back. Chrissy gets the tickets for "Batman" and they go into theater. The theater is dark and advertisements are rolling. They find seats and get comfortable.

"I'm going to the bathroom; you want something from the concession stand?" Symoné asks.

"Cherry slushy, popcorn with lots of butter, please."

Symoné gets up and excuses herself as she crosses over several couples to get out of the aisle.

✳ ✳ ✳

The cashier at the concession stand hands Symoné her order. "Thanks for coming to Whitestone Cinemas. Enjoy the show."

Heading back toward the theater, Symoné sees the guy Chrissy pointed out approaching her.

"What's up, baby girl? Can I talk to you for a minute?" Symoné looks at the guy and smiles.

"Baby girl? My name is Symoné."

"Okay, I'm sorry. My name is T-Bone. Can I talk to you for a minute, Symoné?"

"Depends on what we're going to talk about," Symoné replies.

"What's up after the movies?" T-Bone asks.

"Nothing, I got to get back home to my daughter."

"Is there a man to get back home to, as well? I want no problems."

"You are good, no problems over here."

T-Bone takes a napkin off the counter, pulls a pen out of his inside jacket pocket, and writes his beeper number down, then hands Symoné the napkin. "Hit me up tonight." His beeper beeps. He takes the beeper from the clip on his waistband and looks at the number.

"Excuse me, I gotta go. Call me." T-Bone jogs over to the theater payphone, and Symoné walks back to her movie.

✳ ✳ ✳

Chrissy pulls up and double parks in front of Symoné's building in Striver's Row.

"So, what up with college? When you joining me at Spelman?"

"I don't know. Having a baby changes things. I'm trying to find a job right now. I don't want to keep depending on Mike. College will be there, it's not going anywhere."

"I hear you."

"I'm out, talk to you later," Symoné says, exiting Chrissy's GTI.

Symoné enters her apartment. Mae is asleep on the sofa, and Mykia is sleeping in her playpen. Symoné tiptoes quietly over to the linen closet, takes out a blanket, covers Mae, and goes to bed.

❊ ❊ ❊

It is early in the morning; rush hour. Symoné comes out of the Grand Central train station. There are people in business suits and tourists are everywhere. She has a newspaper in her hands and is checking off a listing. She is wearing a dark-brown skirt, beige silk shirt, a brown tweed sweater, and matching brown shoes and bag. She is dressed very professionally, except for the big, gold, bamboo hoop earrings and an arm full of gold bangles. She walks into an office building on 42nd Street, between Madison and Fifth Avenue.

Symoné walks into CTI Personnel Agency and up to the reception desk.

"I am here for the office assistant position."

"Do you have an appointment?"

"No."

"Where did you last work?"

"I've never worked before."

"Okay, this job is for someone with experience as an office assistant. You may want to check out our temp division next door."

"Thanks," Symoné says and leaves disappointed.

Symoné walks the streets of Midtown and starts to get hot. She takes off her sweater, drapes it over her bag, and walks into another employment agency. The sign on the door reads, Robert Half Office Team.

"Hi, I am here about the office assistant position in the paper."

"Can I have your resume?" the receptionist asks.

"I don't have one."

The receptionist hands her an employment application, a W-4 to fill out, and tests on a clipboard. "I need you to fill out these forms, list any work experience you may have on the application, and complete the written test before you see a counselor."

She observes the other applicants sitting around the agency waiting. She sits on the couch, flips through the paperwork; there's a vocabulary test, a spelling test, a math and reading test. "Damn." She twists up her face and begins filling out the papers.

Symoné finishes the paperwork and hands it to the receptionist.

"Now I need you to take a typing test." The receptionist directs Symoné to a desk, with a typewriter and a standing clipboard with a several typed pages.

"You have five minutes to complete the typing test. When you hear the buzzer that means your time is up. Then put your name and the last four digits of your social at the top of the page and have a seat back in the waiting area. A counselor will then continue with your interview."

"Okay."

"Would you like to take a practice test before beginning?"

"No, thank you. I'd rather just take the test," Symoné says.

The receptionist sets the timer, and Symoné begins typing.

Five minutes later, the buzzer rings. "Time's up," the receptionist says.

Symoné looks disappointed. She gets up from the typewriter and takes a seat back in the reception area. A few minutes later the receptionist calls Symoné back up to the desk.

"Ms. Harris, you scored really low on the typing test for the office assistant position. You may want to practice your typing and come back to test again."

Symoné is back out on the streets. The sun is beaming. Her feet are aching as she walks through Midtown searching for work. There is a guy wearing a billboard, pacing up and down the street, handing out flyers that say, "DAISY JAMES WORKFORCE. We Get You Ready, Find Work & Place Everyone." The guy hands her a flyer, she reads it, and heads over to Daisy James Workforce.

❋ ❋ ❋

Symoné is sitting, finishing up her math test. She hands it to the receptionist and takes a seat in a small reception area with another person. The office is decorated with African art and earth tone colors. There is a water cooler, an instant coffee maker with several flavored gourmet coffees, and biscotti's in a decorated tin can, all on an African drum-shaped table in the corner of the waiting area. She pulls out a stick of gum, pops it into her mouth, and starts chewing.

Daisy James enters the receptionist area. She is a tall, thick Redbone woman, with long, wavy black hair wrapped in navy blue print kente cloth, which matches her wrapped dress. The very pregnant receptionist hands Mrs. James Symoné's application. She puts on her reading glasses that hang from a colorful beaded lanyard around her neck and glances over Symoné's application.

"Symoné Harris?"

Symoné walks over to Mrs. James, smacking on her gum. "Hi, I'm Daisy James," she introduces herself and shakes Symoné's hand. "You can follow me back into my office so we can talk."

They enter Mrs. James's office. It is very plush with African paintings on the walls, along with her degrees and community merit awards. Mrs. James sits behind her desk and looks through Symoné's application and test scores. Symoné sits on the other side of the desk, smacking on her gum, looking around the office. Mrs. James appears to be getting irritated by her gum smacking and cracking.

"Your test results weren't bad, but can be improved upon. I see you just graduated high school, Christ the King, a very good school. So, do you have plans on going to college in the fall?"

"I was accepted to Spellman College, but have to put that on hold for now. I just had a baby and want to focus on raising her."

"I see here on your application you have never worked before, no after school or summer jobs?"

"No."

"Have you been to any other employment agencies?"

"Yes."

"How did things go?"

"Not too well."

"I can help you and want to help you, but you are going to have to brush up on your typing and computer skills." Mrs. James gets up and sits on her desk, facing Symoné. "I'm going to be honest with you, Symoné; first impressions are everything in the corporate world. Your interview clothes are great, but smaller earrings and one or two bangles looks more professional. And next time, leave the chewing gum at home."

Symoné stops chewing her gum. Suddenly, she's embarrassed.

Mrs. James hands Symoné a business card. "I want you to come down to my office for the next two weeks, two hours a day, starting on Monday, practice on the computer, and take the tests again. If you do well, my receptionist is going out on maternity leave and you got yourself a temporary job at seven dollars an hour."

"Wow, thank you, Mrs. James. You don't know how much this means to me. I will see you early Monday morning."

Daisy shakes Symoné's hand. Symoné exits the office with a big smile on her face.

❄ ❄ ❄

Symoné enters the bedroom with a sleepy-eyed Mykia. She takes off Mykia's clothes, puts on her pajamas, and places her into the crib. Symoné looks tired. She sits on the edge of the bed, takes off her shoes, and massages her feet. She reaches over to the nightstand and takes out a picture of her, Mike, and Mykia. Her eyes fill with tears. She puts the picture away, cuts off the light, and leaves the bedroom.

Symoné walks into the living room and turns on the TV. The eleven o'clock news is on. She sits on the sofa and starts going through the mail. She notices the napkin on the coffee table with T-Bone's beeper number. She pages T-Bone. A few moments later the phone rings.

"Hello ... It's Symoné. I met you at the movies the other day ... I would have called you sooner, but ... Tonight? ... Well ... It's going to be kind of hard . . . Let me see what I can do . . . I'll call you back in a few." She hangs up with T-Bone and makes another call. She calls Chrissy, who agrees to watch her daughter. Symoné hangs up and hurries to get dressed.

❊   ❊   ❊

It's raining lightly. T-Bone pulls his BMW in front of Symoné's building and beeps his horn twice. The front door to the brownstone swings open. Symoné is wearing a Gucci tennis dress, with Gucci sneakers, and a matching hooded sweater. She puts the hood over her head, hurries down the stairs, and gets into the car. His pager is beeping. He looks down at the display, it reads 144*911.

"Symoné, something just came up. I have to meet somebody on 144th. So dinner and a movie are out. We can get something to eat, a bottle, and go back to my crib to chill if you want."

"Yeah, that's okay."

❊   ❊   ❊

The rain is coming down hard now. Symoné is sitting in the BMW alone, on the deserted block in front of an old tenement on 144th, between Seventh and Eighth Avenue. She appears to be agitated and looks at her watch. She peers out the foggy windshield and sees T-Bone jogging toward the car. He has a black gym bag in his hand. He gets in the car and puts the bag in the back seat.

"Sorry I took so long, baby."

"I was ready to take your Beamer and go get myself something to eat."

"I swear I'll make it up to you." T-Bone leans over and gives her a kiss on the cheek.

"It's going to take more than that." They laugh.

❊   ❊   ❊

T-Bone parks his BMW on Morningside Park, between West 116th & 117th. Symoné and T-Bone get out of the car. She opens an umbrella, grabs the food, and bottle of Moët. T-Bone lifts the mat up and takes a 9mm from underneath the driver's seat. He puts it into his pants and grabs the black gym bag from the back seat. T-Bone ducks under the umbrella and puts his arm around Symoné. They walk around the corner to his stash house on West 116th Street.

The block is deserted and quiet. Two shifty-looking guys are standing on the stoop in front of a newly renovated tenement, with their hands in their pockets. T-Bone gives them a pound, and he and Symoné continue into the building. The hallway is well lit and clean. They walk down the hall to the last apartment at the end of the hallway. The door has several locks. T-Bone pulls out a hand full of keys and opens the door. Two guys, Emo and Peanut, hurry to the door with their guns drawn.

"I got friend with me yo, put the nines away. You goin' scare baby girl away," T-Bone says sternly.

Emo and Peanut tuck their guns back into the waist of their pants.

"Damn, you almost got your wig split," Peanut says.

"Cuzzo, why didn't you give me a heads-up and let me know you were coming through?" Emo asks.

"I thought ya niggas were going on Jerry Wells's boat ride," T-Bone responds.

"The streets is calling, cuzzo, gotta get this money," Emo replies.

"I hear you loud and clear, son," T-Bone says and then introduces Symoné. "This is my future wife, Symoné. And this is my cuz, Emo, and my boy, Peanut."

"What up?" Peanut and Emo respond simultaneously.

"Hi," Symoné says.

They all walk down the hall toward the living room. The lights are dim. The carpet is stained and needs to be vacuumed. The furniture is second hand. Above the sofa is a big-framed picture of Malcolm X looking out window and holding a rifle. There are other pictures on the walls of Hip Hop artists, N.W.A., Run D.M.C., Public Enemy, Queen Latifah, Salt-N-Pepa, and several pictures are of Janet Jackson. A large floor model television is in the living room, tuned to the SportsChannel. A VCR is on the floor next to dozens of bootleg videotapes. The windows' black vertical blinds are closed.

"Symoné, have a seat, eat your food."

"I'm good."

"I need to holla at my boyz. I'll be with you in a minute." T-Bone walks into the kitchen with Emo and Peanut, gym bag in hand.

Symoné has a seat on the edge of the sofa. She looks around the half-lit room and is uneasy.

❈ ❈ ❈

T-Bone walks into the kitchen and puts the black gym bag on the large glass table. There are soda cans and beer bottles on the table, along with different sized crack vials, bags of crack, a counting machine, stacks of money wrapped in rubber bands, a 357 Snub Nose, and Desert Eagle.

"Where you met girlfriend at? She's a hottie," Peanut says.

"No doubt, you get a ten for that one," Emo adds.

"I get a ten on all the girls I bring back to the crib," T-Bone says, smirking.

"The last one you brought back was looking kind of rough around the edges, cuz," Emo admits.

"You buggin', her face might have been a six, but that body was the bomb," T-Bone says. He looks around the kitchen and notices how filthy it is. The sink is full of dirty dishes, the trashcan is over flowing, pizza boxes and beer cans are piled up next to the trashcan. "Damn niggas, ya'll could have cleaned up some."

"We were waiting for your ass to come and do it," Emo replies, as he and Peanut laugh.

"Yeah, all right nigga. It ain't goin' be so funny when your cheddar is short at the end of the week, and I cut your ass off," T-Bone retorts.

"Com'on cuzzo, I'm playing. Why you always so serious? You know I got you. Shit just got busy on the streets, and we didn't have time to do it," Emo explains.

T-Bone opens the gym bag, takes out stacks of money, and puts it on the table. Emo and Peanut take the rubber bands off the stacks and start counting. He leaves the kitchen and goes back into the living room, where Symoné is waiting.

"I'm ready to go home, T-Bone. I'm not feeling this."

T-Bone takes Symoné by the hand. "Relax, baby. It's all good. Come on. Let's go in the room and chill." He grabs the bag of food and Moët, and they head into the bedroom.

The bedroom is dark and the blue light is on. The shades are drawn. Most of the light is coming from the television on the dresser. There are very exotic framed pictures on the walls of half naked, voluptuous African American and Latino women. There is a large mirror attached to the ceiling above the queen-sized bed, which is covered with satin sheets. There is a sneaker box with money stacked on top of the bed. The dresser directly in front of the bed has a camcorder on it, a couple of sneaker boxes, and empty champagne bottles.

"Have a seat, relax, take off your sweater," T-Bone suggests.

Symoné takes off her sweater and sits on the bed. She is extremely nervous.

T-Bone walks over to the dresser, puts the take-out and Moët down next to the camcorder. He picks up the sneaker box, puts the money in the box, and opens the closet door. There is an AK-47 in the corner of the closet, with boxes of bullets. He puts the money on the top shelf with the other sneaker boxes, next to four bricks of cocaine, and closes the closet door.

"Symoné, give me your sweater so I can hang it up." She hands him the sweater. He walks over to the bedroom door, pulls it back. There is another AK-47 behind the door.

"Ya'll have guns everywhere. What's up with that?"

"Just precaution, you never know."

"You sell drugs out of here?"

"Nah, this is my stash house, where I lay my head from time to time. You have nothing to worry about, baby girl, you are in good hands."

T-Bone hangs his jacket and Symoné's sweater on the hooks behind the bedroom door. He then walks over to the dresser and pours himself and Symoné a drink. Before he hands Symoné her cup, he discreetly presses the record button on the camcorder. He walks over to the bed and hands Symoné one of the cups. "Maybe this will help you relax a little more," he says.

"Thanks." Symoné takes the Moët and drinks.

T-Bone takes his 9mm and pager and puts them on the nightstand by the bed, next to the portable CD player and mini speakers. He presses play on the CD player. It's Surface singing, "Shower Me With Your Love".

Symoné's nervousness turns to sadness when she hears the song. It takes her back to prom night with Mike.

T-Bone notices Symoné's mood has changed. "What's the matter? You seem kind of distant."

"That song is taking me back. It's been tough since me and my ex broke up."

"You need a job?"

"I went on an interview earlier today and I may have something lined up at minimum wage."

"That's peanuts. You want the chance to make some real money?"

"Doing what?"

"Does it really matter? It's tax free, pays the bills, and pays more than a minimum wage job that's gonna have you busting your ass eight hours a day for peanuts."

"Sounds tempting, but it depends on what it is."

"It's on you. I put it out there. Now, let's forget about all that stuff and enjoy the night." T-Bone takes the Moët bottle off the dresser and refills Symoné's cup. She drinks.

"I see you play ball. You have a lot of trophies."

"I used to play. Now I have a team that plays in the Rucker and at the Cage on West 4th." T-Bone sees Symoné's cup is getting empty and refills it.

"Are you trying to get me drunk and take advantage of me?" she asks with a seductive grin on her face. The Moët is sneaking up on her and she is feeling a little tipsy.

"Nah, I'm just trying to show you a good time."

"It's getting warm in here. Could you open a window?"

T-Bone gets up and opens the window.

"Damn, I'm really feeling this Moët. It just snuck up on me. Here, take this." Symoné hands T-Bone her empty cup and he puts it on the nightstand.

She is very tipsy and sleepy. "I'm feeling a little tired. Maybe I should call it a night. I don't want to fall asleep on you."

"You can stay the night if you want."

"I don't know. I have to get back to my daughter."

"When the last time you been out and just enjoyed yourself?"

"It has been a long time."

"Exactly," T-Bone assures her. "So lay back and enjoy yourself."

T-Bone gently leans Symoné back on the bed. He starts nibbling on her ears and neck, as he fondles her breasts, then slowly moves his hand up her dress.

Symoné is tipsy and starts giggling. "No, T-Bone, stop. It's too soon." She pulls his hand from under her dress.

Come on, Symoné, let me make you feel good," T-Bone pleads. He slides down toward Symoné's thighs, slowly works his head up her dress, and feels the dampness between her legs. She is moaning and wiggling around on the bed. He grabs hold of her rear to keep her from moving away, as he pleasures her inner thighs, moving further and further toward her center.

He uses his tongue to move the crotch of her panties to the side. She is soaking wet. The scent of her wetness and moans are getting him extremely excited. The louder she moans, the more he wants her.

T-Bone tries to muffle the sounds by putting one hand over her mouth. He takes off his pants and kneels on the bed over Symoné and props a pillow under her head. He rubs his member across her lips.

"Kiss it for me."

"No, stop" she says and turns her face.

"Pleasssseeeee, Symoné. Do this for me, just this one time."

Symoné hesitates, then gives his member a peck.

"Damn baby, you have some soft lips. Now put your tongue on it for me."

Symoné slightly opens her mouth and puts the tip of her tongue on the head of T-Bone's member. He takes his member and moves it around the tip of her tongue.

"Yeah baby, just like that," T-Bone says as he softly caresses her center. Her center is getting wetter and she starts to open her mouth more to take him further in. He becomes impatient, grabs her head with both hands and begins thrusting his growing member further into her mouth, which causes her to gag. He pulls out and puts on the condom. Symoné is so intoxicated from the Moët, she can barely move. She lies helpless on the bed as he removes her clothes.

He kneels back on the floor and pulls Symoné back down toward the edge. His tongue finds her wet center. "Ohhhhhhhh, Mike."

T-Bone stops for a moment when he hears Symoné call him Mike. He twists up his face, but then continues to pleasure her.

"Put it in me, now."

T-Bone turns Symoné on her stomach and props two pillows under her hips. He slides his member into the dampness between her legs. It excites him and he delves deeper into her with each rhythmic push. Symoné is trying to get away, but he pulls her by her waist, back down onto his shaft, thrusting in and out, fast and hard. Symoné is a great deal of pain, but at the same time she is aroused and the wetness of her womanhood spills out and down her inner thigh. He takes advantage of the opportunity and takes off the condom, sliding his member into her rear in one swift motion. She screams out for a moment and passes out. He moans with delight, thrusting himself wildly inside her.

"Damn, this ass is tight," he blurts out. Sweat is dripping off his face onto Symoné's back, as he thrusts with great force and purpose. He pulls out before he releases, grabs hold of his member, strokes it quickly, and lets out a loud moan. He collapses on the bed and passes out next to Symoné.

❋   ❋   ❋

A couple hours later, T-Bone's beeper is beeping back to back. He wakes up, reaches over Symoné, who is still knocked out cold on the bed, and grabs the beeper off the nightstand. It reads 122*911. It's six in the morning. He slaps Symoné on the butt. "Wake up, Symoné. I have to make a run." He drags himself out of bed, walks over to the dresser, and stops the camcorder.

Symoné is having a hard time getting out of bed. She has a hangover and a bad headache. "Damn, what the hell happened last night? My head is killing me."

"Symoné, I got to go. Com'on and get dress." He hands Symoné her tennis dress. She can't seem to get it on. T-Bone helps her put the dress over her head and zips up the back. She grabs her panties at the head of the bed and puts them on and then her sneakers.

T-Bone walks over to the door and grabs his jacket and Symoné's sweater. He hands her the sweater and grabs his nine and beeper off the nightstand. When she finally gets her sweater on, they leave.

❊ ❊ ❊

It is pouring out. T-Bone stops at the doorway of the building. He has his black gym bag across his shoulder and an umbrella. Symoné is extremely disheveled. He gives her the umbrella and takes a stack of money out his pocket, peels off five twenty-dollar bills and hands it to her.

"What's this for?"

"I need you to take a cab."

"It's pouring out here."

"I can't take you home. I have some business to take care of. I'll call you later." T-Bone puts the collar up on his jacket, hurries down the stairs, and up the block toward his BMW on Morningside Drive.

Symoné is upset as she watches T-Bone hurry down the block. She opens the umbrella, exits the building into the pouring rain, and tries to flag down a cab.

❊ ❊ ❊

Symoné enters her apartment and closes the door. She is soaking wet. The sound of the door closing wakes Chrissy, who was sleeping on the sofa. Chrissy looks at the time on her watch.

"Girl, what the hell happened to you? Where you been? It's after seven in the morning."

"Could you just lower your voice a little, I have a migraine." Symoné walks over to the dining room table, sits, and lays her head on the table. Chrissy gets up off the sofa and walks over to Symoné, lifting her head up and looking into her face.

"Girl, you tore-up? I hope it was worth it."

Symoné gets up and hurries over to the sink to throw up.

"Damn, you feel better now?"

"Hell no," Symoné says and walks over to Chrissy to give her a hug. "Chrissy, please, could you stay a little while longer and watch Mykia. I just need a little sleep." Symoné is still a little tipsy. She kisses Chrissy on the cheek. "You the best friend any girl can ask for. Love you, girl."

"Okay. Now go take your drunk ass to the bathroom and shower."

Symoné stumbles out of the kitchen. Chrissy shakes her head and smiles as Symoné bumps into the furniture on her way to the shower.

❋ ❋ ❋

Kharizma is cozy in Mike's arms on her designer, queen size, canopy bed with hanging red, silk drapes. They are asleep under the satin, zebra print sheets and black comforter.

The sunlight peaks through the black vertical blinds, hitting Mike's face and he wakes up. He stares at the sunlight for a moment with squinted eyes, gently lifting Kharizma's head and arms and slides out of bed. He walks over to the window, partially opens the blinds, and looks out at the sunrise. He is thinking about Symoné and Mykia. Kharizma wakes and gets out of bed. She is wearing a sexy red teddy. She walks over to Mike, wraps her arms around his waist, and kisses him on the back of the neck.

"You up early. Is everything all right?"

"Yeah."

"No, it's not. You feeling guilty about us hooking up?."

"Nah, for what? It over between Symoné and I."

"You sure?"

Mike turns, puts his arms around Kharizma, and gives her a kiss.

Kharizma takes Mike's hand and guides him back to bed, cuddling underneath him. He wraps his arm around her. She smiles and closes her eyes. He has sadness in his, a tear falling as he stares off into space.

1990

CHOICES WE MAKE

· ·

CHAPTER 9

Spring Break, March 1990

It's been a few of months since Mike and Symoné broke up. She has been seeing T-Bone off and on. The telephone rings. She wakes and looks over at the digital clock on the nightstand; it reads 4:00 AM. She looks over at Mykia in the crib. She picks up the phone and whispers into the receiver, so she does not wake her.

"Hello?"

"What up?"

"Who is this?" Symoné asks.

"Oh, you forgot about me already?"

"T-Bone?"

"What up, baby girl?"

"Where you been?"

"Getting this money. Ready to do the same?"

"Do you know what time it is?"

"Money don't sleep, baby. Could you get a babysitter this afternoon for a few hours?"

"I guess so."

"I'll come through sometime this afternoon."

"Yeah, okay," she says and hangs up the telephone. Symoné tries to go back to sleep, but is unable to. She gets out of bed, walks over to the crib, and checks on Mykia instead.

❊ ❊ ❊

Fisher is unshaved, sitting on the recliner in the living room, watching the news. He is drinking heavily and half way through the six-pack of Miller High Life. The news anchor's report has attracted his attention.

"Another big story we are following today, NYPD Superintendent, Anthony Coleman, wasted no time yesterday and suspended several veteran detectives without pay . . ."

Fisher gets up and stumbles over to the TV with a bottle in his hand, turns up the volume, sits back down on the edge of the recliner, and continues drinking his beer.

". . . pending an investigation into alleged misconduct. We will bring you more updates on this report as they come in. And now, a former Bronx principal and reverend accused of raping two girls and impregnating one of them while they were minors at the school . . ."

Fisher is agitated by the news report. He flings the open beer bottle at the TV. The bottle shatters the screen. Glass is everywhere.

Mae, dressed in her nurse's uniform, comes running down the stairs into the living room. She looks at the broken television and glass, exclaiming, "What the hell is going on?"

"NUTH-EING!" he screams.

"Jack, I think you have had enough. And who drinks beer at seven o'clock in the morning?" Mae attempts to take the unopened and empty beer bottles off the end table.

Fisher becomes extremely angry. He jumps up off the recliner and grabs Mae by the collar of her nurse's uniform, shaking her up. "I'MA ROOOWN ASS MANN! WHAT DA ELL YA TAL-IN BOUT?"

Mae is in shock and pulls away from Fisher. "All this drinking has you going crazy."

Fisher snatches one of the beer bottles she is holding and accidently hits her in the bottle in her mouth.

"OUCH!" She yells out in pain, stumbling backwards, dropping all the bottles. Her mouth is bleeding and immediately starts to swell.

"NOOW LOOO-KU WHA-CHA DUUN MAA-AY MEEEE DOO WOO-MANN!"

Mae hurries out of the living room over to the kitchen and gets ice to put on her lip and Fisher, drunk and sweaty, stumbles over to the guest room, opens the door, and slams it closed behind him.

❋   ❋   ❋

It is late in the afternoon. Mae's lip is swollen and she is cleaning up the last of the broken glass on the floor when the doorbell rings. She answers and it is Symoné and her granddaughter, Mykia. Mae grabs Mykia out of Symoné's arms, carries her in the house, and smothers her with kisses.

"How's Nana's baby?"

Symoné follows them in the house, places Mykia's diaper bag on the coffee table, and sits. She notices the broken television.

"What happened to the TV?"

Mae sits down on the sofa next to Symoné and is bouncing Mykia on her lap.

"A little accident. Jack was drinking a little too much."

Symoné notices Mae lip. "And what happened to your lip?"

"Long story. Did you remember to pack a change of clothes? I'm taking Mykia to the park today."

"Yeah, I did. Where's Jack?"

"He's in the room asleep."

Symoné looks at her watch. "At two o'clock in the afternoon? You sure everything is all right?"

"Of course, why wouldn't it be?"

"I'm just asking." Symoné gets up from the sofa and gives Mae and Mykia a kiss. "If you need me, call. I have a few things to do, but I will be back tonight to pick up Mykia." Symoné walks toward the front door and looks back at her mother one more time, with concern, before she walks out the door.

❋   ❋   ❋

Symoné is in her apartment, tidying up the living room. The doorbell rings. She opens the door for T-Bone. He has a backpack on and is carrying a large shopping bag. He attempts to give Symoné a kiss on the mouth and she turns her face, giving him her cheek instead. She turns and walks over to the sofa, her hourglass shape complimented by an acid-washed mini-skirt and a tube-top that exposes her belly button. T-Bone watches her with a smile on his face.

"Oh, it's like that?" T-Bone says, closing the door behind him.

"What else is it like? I haven't seen you in weeks." Symoné retorts, as she walks over to the sofa and sits down with her arms folded.

T-Bone puts his things down and gives Symoné a hug. "I've been busy getting this money. Don't be mad at me. I'm here now."

"Whatever."

"You ready to get this money?"

"You here, right?"

"Damn baby girl, you sexy as hell." T-Bone leans over and Symoné allows him to kiss her on the lips, and then he tries to slide his hands up her skirt, but she pushes his hand away.

"I don't think so, you got to earn it."

"I hear you, no problem. You wanna come with me to Atlantic City this weekend?"

"I'll think about it."

"Don't think too long. Now let's get in this kitchen and go to work."

T-Bone picks up his bags and follows Symoné into the kitchen. He puts the backpack on the table, puts the shopping bag in the chair, and takes out a scale, a large glass cutting board, two surgical masks, and three different sizes of crack bottles, baking soda, and a half-key of coke.

"Symoné, would it be a problem if I asked you to hold this backpack here? I'll pay you just to hold it." T-Bone hands her the backpack. Symoné opens it and looks in. It's two keys of coke.

"I don't know, T-Bone. I don't mind making a few dollars, but holding drugs in my house?"

"You good, I got you. Who's going to know the bricks are here, but me and you? You don't have a man coming in and out your apartment, do you?"

"Nah, but . . ."

T-Bone reaches in his pocket and hands Symoné ten crisp hundred-dollar bills. She takes the money and the backpack and leaves the kitchen. She comes back to find T-Bone drinking a can of soda he took out the refrigerator.

"You really making yourself comfortable."

"I thought we were good like that, baby girl. My bad." T-Bone laughs and slaps Symoné on her butt. "I need you to get a large pot and boil some water."

Symoné obliges.

"Okay, the water's boiling. Now, put on your mask."

Symoné puts on her surgical mask and watches everything that T-Bone does carefully. He picks up the coke from the table.

"This is a half a key of coke, worth about thirteen-thousand on the streets, and a lot more when we mix it up into crack."

T-Bone puts the coke and baking soda in the pot and then stirs the pot slowly in a circular motion, until the powder is hard. He takes the rock out of the pot, drains the excess water, puts it in the freezer for a few minutes, and then takes it out. He puts the crack onto a glass cutting board; shows Symoné how to weigh, cut, and bottle it.

The telephone rings. Symoné, "Hello?"

"Hello, Ms. Harris? It's Mrs. Daisy James from the employment agency."

"Hello, Mrs. James. I was going to call you."

"I haven't seen you since we last spoke. Are you still interested in the job?"

"Yes, I am. Something has come up and I can't work right now."

T-Bone is trying to distract Symoné. While she talks on the phone, he stands behind her grinding on her butt as she fills the crack bottles. She turns around and gives him a dirty look, putting her hand over the receiver. "Chill," she whispers harshly.

"Well, if you want, you can still come down to my office and use the computer to brush up on your skills."

"Thank you so much for the opportunity." Symoné hangs up the phone.

"What's wrong with you? I was taking care of business."

"This is your business now." T-Bone kisses her on the back of the neck and they continue to bottle the rocks.

❄ ❄ ❄

Symoné is parked in front of Esplanade Gardens, waiting for Chrissy in a brand new white Saab 900 Turbo Convertible, blasting Jody Watley's, "Real Love". Chrissy comes out of the building and is surprised to see Symoné in a brand new car.

"Sup, this is butter. What nigga you pimpin'?" Chrissy gets into the car.

"I'm not pimpin' nobody. Remember that guy from the Whitestone? I've been kind of seeing him."

"That lame ass nigga that had you take a cab in the rain?"

"Whatever." Symoné pulls off and they cruise up Adam Clayton Powell, Jr. Boulevard, toward the George Washington Bridge.

"Long time no see. Where you been? How's Mykia and the new job going?"

"Damn bitch, one question at a time. Mykia is good. She's getting big and spoiled. Wants me to hold her all day, and I didn't take the temp job."

"What?"

"I'm all right. T-Bone is helping me out."

"I thought you weren't tryin' to depend on a man."

"I'm not. I'm working for mines."

"Doing what?"

"If I tell you this, you better not tell anybody."

"Who am I going to tell?"

"Eddie. And then Eddie is going to tell Mike."

"I am not going to tell anybody, including Eddie."

"I'm cooking up crack for T-Bone."

"What? Girl, is you buggin'? You cook up that shit around Mykia?"

"Nah, I take her to my mom's house during the day when I'm working."

"Yo, that lame ass nigga don't give a fuck about you or your daughter. If he did, he wouldn't be doing that shit in your house. He is using your ass."

"We are using each other. I'm not looking to marry T-Bone. This is sweet for now. It helps me pay the bills and take care of Mykia. We don't want for nothing and don't have to ask nobody for nothing. Mykia and I are good."

"You fucking him?"

"From time to time."

"Whatever you do, just be careful, girl. I'm really not feeling this nigga."

"I'll be careful. Now stop worrying so much and let's go shopping."

Symoné pulls up and parks inside the Paramus Park Mall. They get out the car and notice Mike's Wrangler in the lot.

"Isn't that Mike's Jeep?" Chrissy asks.

"Looks like it," Symoné says.

"When the last time you heard from Mike?" Chrissy inquires.

"It's been a minute," Symoné replies.

"You know he still asks about you."

"Yeah, he's always coming by my moms and dropping money off. How's he doing?"

"Mike's doing good. He's the man up at USC. The lead scorer on the team and the reason why the Tar Heels made it into the NCAA Championship."

Symoné and Chrissy are half way to the front door of the mall when they run into Mike. He is with Kharizma and she is carrying several Macy's shopping bags.

"Wow, really, Mike? All the girls you could be with, and you're here with her," Chrissy blurts.

Kharizma puts her hand on her hip, looking at Chrissy up and down.

"Yeah, um," Mike stammers and hands Kharizma his car keys. "Here, why don't you go and put your things in the car. I'll be there in a minute."

"Okay baby," Kharizma says with a grin, as she takes the keys and walks away.

"Skeezer," Chrissy mumbles under her breath. Kharizma hears her, turns around, rolls her eyes at Chrissy, flips her the bird, and continues on toward the Jeep.

Mike gives Symoné a hug and kiss on the cheek. "How have you and Mykia been?

"Good."

"So, when you started messing around with that Skeezer?" Chrissy interrupts.

"She's just a friend. She needed a ride to the mall, that's all. So how you been, Symoné? I've been trying to reach you. Why haven't you called me back? I want to see you and Mykia."

"I've been very busy, like I see you've been."

"It's not like that, I . . ."

"You don't have to explain nothing to me, Mike."

"I want to talk to you. Could we meet up tonight or could I come by?"

"I don't think that's a good idea. I'll call you."

"Okay," Mike says and gives her a hug. He catches Symoné off guard when he kisses her on the lips. She kisses him back.

"Take care, Mike," Symoné says.

"See you later, Mike," Chrissy adds.

Symoné is overwhelmed with sadness and her eyes become watery as she watches Mike walk away.

DÉJÀ VU

· ·

CHAPTER 10

It's the weekend; Symoné is at the Trump Plaza Hotel and Casino with T-Bone, his cousin Emo, and Emo's guest, Puerto Rican Lola. T-Bone and Emo have connecting ocean view, jacuzzi suites. The group is lounging around, having a good time, talking, drinking, smoking weed, and listening to music.

Emo and Lola are lying on the rug, face-up. Lola is in a very sexy and revealing outfit; a black silk, mini-skirt and a black see-through chiffon tied at the waist to show off her bare firm breast and perfectly-shaped belly button. Emo is drinking from a champagne bottle. Lola opens her mouth and lets him pour the champagne in. He pours a little too much, causing the champagne to spill out of her mouth, down her chin. He starts tasting the champagne on her wet lips. She opens her mouth and kisses him with hungry urgency. He rips open her top and sucks up the leftover champagne, as he squeezes her firm 36 double D breasts. Lola puts her hands down his pants and starts massaging his member.

Symoné is annoyed by their public display. T-Bone is getting aroused and his member is bulging through his pants. He turns and sticks his wet tongue in Symoné's ear, cupping her breast and gently squeezing. Symoné pushes his hands off and T-Bone becomes agitated.

"Sup, Symoné? We supposed to be having fun."

"Fun watching your cuz and some skeezer get their freak on?" Symoné snaps.

"That shit doesn't turn you on, even a little?"

"Hell no, I don't feel like sitting up here in the suite. I'm all dressed up and want to go to the casino."

"Chill, in a minute," T-Bone replies.

He pulls a folded, crisp hundred-dollar bill, some coke, and a credit card from his pocket. He puts the bill on the coffee table in front of the sofa, opens it up, and uses the credit card to break the small rocks into powder. Then he takes his keys and uses the end of it to snort the coke. He picks up more and puts it to Symoné's nose.

"Want some?"

"Nah, I'm good."

"I'll take it," Lola says eagerly, as she pushes Emo off her, hurrying over to T-Bone. She bends over the table, exposing her lace bra and sniffs the coke off the end of T-Bone's key.

"Damn, this shit is good," says Lola.

"Want some more?" offers T-Bone.

Lola nods her head yes and T-Bone empties the rest out on the coffee table. He uses the credit card to move the coke into lines, rolls up the bill, and hands it to Lola. She places one end inside her nostril, presses her other nostril flat with her other hand, and inhales the coke. She passes the bill back to T-Bone. Emo comes over to the table and joins them. Lola hands him the rolled up bill and he snorts from the table. Emo takes some of the coke off the table and sprinkles it between Lola's naked breasts, then snorts it. T-Bone joins in the fun and starts snorting lines off Lola.

Lola is enjoying all the attention, laughing and rubbing their heads between her breasts as they suckle and snort the coke. Lola gets up off the carpeted floor, moving very provocatively to the music playing in the suite.

T-Bone and Emo are getting more turned on watching Lola's firm, tight body moving and dancing. Her long, black curly hair brushes against her round, plump rear. Emo joins Lola on the floor, holding her close and cupping her rear with both hands, while kissing her all over her face and neck.

T-Bone gets up from the sofa and gets his camcorder from his luggage to start recording Lola and Emo. T-Bone joins in the dance session. They have Lola in between them, like a sandwich. Lola bends over and rubs her rear on T-Bone's bulging member, then pulls out Emo's member and begins pleasuring him. She is very high, giggling and laughing loudly. Lola looks over at Symoné, reaches her hand out and licks her lips, gesturing for her to come join the party. Symoné is upset by the porn session, and looks at Lola with disgust. She finally gets up from the sofa.

"T-Bone, I'm out. You coming with me to the casino?"

T-Bone does not look at Symoné as she talks to him, and does not notice how upset she is. His focus and attention is on Lola's rear, as he records her grinding on him. "I'll meet you down there."

"I need some money."

Still focused on Lola's rear and recording, T-Bone reaches in his pocket and pulls out a knot of twenties and hands it to Symoné.

❋ ❋ ❋

Symoné is dressed in a strapless, black sequin dress, just above the knee and five-inch satin pumps. She sits in a high chair at the high rollers slot machines, downstairs at the Trump Plaza Hotel and Casino. She is on her second apple martini. She inserts several twenties into the slot machine and is playing five dollars per spin. She keeps glancing down at her watch. She appears bored and is not having a good time, even though she is up a thousand dollars.

Craig Little is also in the casino with his lieutenants, Willow and Dobie. Symoné does not notice Craig Little approaching from the rear.

"So I guess it is a myth, high roller slots do have a nice little payout."

Symoné turns and sees Craig Little and a big smile spreads across her face. "So, we meet again," Symoné responds.

"Yeah, they say the third time's the charm. So, what you goin' do?"

Symoné blushes. Craig Little introduces her to Willow and Dobie.

"So, this is the young lady that keeps slipping away," Willow comments.

"Like butter," replies Craig Little.

"She is gorgeous, for sure," Dobie compliments.

"Thank you," says Symoné.

"Why you sitting up here at the slot machine all dressed up by yourself?" Craig Little asks.

"Long story," Symoné replies.

"You can tell me later over breakfast."

"Breakfast?"

"Yeah, unless you have somewhere else to be?" Craig Little responds.

"No, nowhere else."

"We're on our way to the Black Jack table; I can use a lucky charm." Craig Little holds his hand out for Symoné. She smiles, takes his hand and her winnings, and leaves with Craig Little and his soldiers.

Craig Little escorts Symoné into the high rollers Black Jack lounge and sits at a table with a minimum bet of a hundred dollars and maximum of five thousand. Craig pulls a chair next to him for Symoné to have a seat, while his soldiers, Willow and Dobie, stand in the background, talking and smoking cigars.

Symoné is impressed as she looks around at the décor and lavish atmosphere in the high rollers lounge. There are two security guards at the entrance and very tall, attractive women hosts, serving drinks in uniformed low-cut, mini dresses and black pumps. Big money is being betted at the tables. One of them is a well-dressed white woman with blue eyes and blonde hair. She's playing with stacks of chips, surrounded by wealthy Japanese and Arab men dressed in traditional garb.

"A Harvey's on the rocks and a bottle of Dom Perignon for the lady," Craig Little says to the hostess, as he gives the dealer ten thousand for chips. The dealer is a tall, model-like female dressed in a black cocktail dress, with a no-nonsense look. The bet starts with five hundred. The dealer deals. Craig Little's first card is an ace. The dealer puts her first card face down, and then deals everyone at the table a second card. Craig Little gets another ace and then splits the aces into two hands, hoping to double his winnings. The dealer faces her second card up and it's a king. She deals Craig Little a nine on his first hand, giving him twenty, and a queen on his second hand, giving him Black Jack. The dealer pays him fifteen hundred on the second hand. When she faces her second card up, it's an eight. Craig Little beats the dealer again, winning another thousand dollars.

At this point, Craig Little is on a winning streak, playing hand after hand, betting higher and higher. He plays for several hours and triples his money. Suddenly, Symoné gets up and whispers in his ear. "I got to go, but I'll talk to you later."

Craig Little looks at his watch. "What about breakfast?"

"I don't want to stop your winning streak."

"Nah, can't let you slip away again, and I've tripled my money, I'm good."

"I'll go get my things from the room and meet you out front."

Craig takes his winnings and they leave the Black Jack lounge.

❊ ❊ ❊

Symoné enters her suite. The music is loud. There are champagne bottles and glasses everywhere, coke and weed on the table, and a trail of a woman›s garments on the carpet. She turns off the music and hears more music coming from Emo's adjoining suite. She goes into her bedroom to gather her things. T-Bone is not in the room, and the bed has not been slept in. She gathers up her bag and exits the suite. She opens the front door to leave, but decides to let T-Bone know. She heads over to Emo's adjoining suite and goes in. No one is in the front room. She hears voices and moaning coming from the bedroom.

"Slow down, baby. I don't want to cum yet."

"This fat ass is tight, mmmm."

One of the voices sound like T-Bone. She frowns and quietly walks toward the bedroom, the sounds of a woman moaning getting louder.

"Yeah papi, fuck me in the ass, like that, papi."

The bedroom door is closed. Symoné puts her ear to the door and listens.

"Fuck, my battery is running low," says T-Bone.

Symoné slowly opens the door and peeks in the bedroom. T-Bone is standing in front of a king size bed, with his pants down to his knees, videotaping Lola. She's completely naked on her knees and hands, with his member in her mouth, as Emo kneels half-naked behind her.

"What the fuck, you nasty-ass dogs?" Symoné exclaims as she pushes the door open.

The sound of the doorknob hitting the back wall startles T-Bone, who drops his camcorder. "Shit."

Symoné turns and leaves the room. T-Bone pulls up his pants, picks up his camcorder, and hurries behind her. Lola laughs and then moans with delight as Emo continues pounding his member into her rear. "Yeah papi, faster, I'm about to bust."

❋　❋　❋

Symoné is outside the suite, waiting for the elevator, when the door to her suite flies opens. T-Bone scurries toward her.

"Symoné, sup? Where are you going?"

"Where you think I'm going? Home!"

"I'm saying, that trick don't mean anything to me."

Symoné is ignores T-Bone and presses the elevator button repeatedly. The elevator door opens and Symoné steps in with her bag. T-Bone grabs her arm and tries to pull her out of the elevator. She does not see Craig Little, Willow, and Dobie in the elevator.

"Sup?" Craig Little says, as Willow and Dobie reach under their shirts, putting their hands on the nines in their waistband.

Symoné looks up and sees Craig and a smile spreads across her face. "Craig, it's cool."

T-Bone looks surprised when he sees Craig Little in the elevator and lets Symoné's arm go. "Little?"

Dobie stands in front of the elevator door and holds it open, with his hand still on his nine.

"Yeah, sup? Problem with the lady?" Craig Little asks.

"Nah, we cool. Just need to speak with her a minute," T-Bone explains.

"You want to talk with him?" Craig Little asks Symoné. She does not say a word and steps into the elevator with her bag. Dobie stops holding the door and backs up into the elevator. Symoné presses the close button. T-Bone stands outside the elevator, starring at Symoné as the door closes in his face.

LOVER'S TRIANGLE

. . . .

CHAPTER 11

A couple of months after the incident at the Trump Plaza, Symoné no longer cooks and bottles crack for T-Bone. She's Craig Little's woman, living in the suburbs of New Jersey, and being taken care of very well. It's Memorial Day weekend. They are dressed to impress and going to the club.

The Omni Park hotel is crowded. New York's hottest DJ, the legendary Reggie Wells is on the turntable and has the party jumping. Everybody that is somebody is at the party; drug dealers with their wives or main girls, celebrities, groupies, and wannabes. Only top shelf liquor is being served at the bar. The VIP section is popping bottles and drinking champagne like water, as the scent from Cuban cigars fill the air.

Mike is in the V.I.P. lounge with Eddie, Chrissy, and Hershey.

T-Bone is also at the party with his cousin, Emo, and his friends Peanut, Quincy, and Scooter. They're drinking at the bar. Peanut sees Symoné walk into the party with Craig Little and his entourage.

"Yo T-Bone, check it out. Ain't that your girl with Little?" Peanut asks.

T-Bone turns around and sees Symoné. "Fuck that hoe." He turns back to the bar and orders a shot.

"Damn homie, I'm sorry. Didn't mean to upset you," Peanut responds.

"Upset what? Fuck that trick," T-Bone retorts, and drinks the shot and orders another one.

"Damn cuz, that trick really got you fucked up," Emo says.

"I've never known Little to talk to no tricks or hoes," Scooter adds.

"Little about that paper. I never seen a girl on his arm, and he's holding that dime close," Quincy comments.

"She all right," says T-Bone.

"Why you hating, homie? What happened, Little stole your girl?" Quincy asks sarcastically.

"That nigga paper long enough, too," Scooter chimes. The guys laugh. Emo tries to hold back from laughing, but he grins and shakes his head.

T-Bone is getting upset about the guys clowning him. "Nobody stole nothing. That hoe was just another piece of ass."

"It looks like she meant more than that, the way you putting down those shots, homie," Emo says.

"Yeah, that blood vessel in your forehead keeps getting bigger and bigger every time you talk about homegirl," Scooter continues.

"Fuck ya' niggas," T-Bone exclaims.

The guys look at T-Bone's big vein pulsing from the middle of his forehead. They all start laughing uncontrollably, except T-Bone.

"I got that hoe on tape, sucking my dick and banging the shit outta her. I got that freak bitch taking backshots in the ass, taking my cum all in her face and mouth. Now that nigga kissing the hoe that wrapped her lips around my dick," T-Bone says in anger, and orders a Bacardi and Coke.

"Word homie, I hear that," Quincy says, taking a sip of his drink.

"Damn, homegirl get down like that?" Scooter asks as he signals the bartender.

"Yeah, she gets down like that. I'm out, need to find me another bitch around here to turn the fuck out," T-Bone says, and puts a hundred-dollar bill in the tip jar. He takes his Bacardi and Coke and gets lost in the crowd.

❄ ❄ ❄

Craig Little is holding Symoné's hand as they walk toward the V.I.P. lounge with Willow and Dobie. There are two big bodyguards standing in front of the roped-off V.I.P. section. When Craig Little approaches, the big muscular bouncers immediately open the rope and show him much love.

Chrissy is in a corner on a plush sofa with Mike, Eddie, and his entourage. She sees Symoné enter the V.I.P. area and she smiles.

"Hey baby, I'll be back," Chrissy whispers to Eddie. "I think I see Symoné coming into V.I.P."

When Mike hears this, he gets distracted from the basketball conversation with the fellas and his attention is immediately drawn to the people coming into the V.I.P. lounge. He sees Symoné holding onto Craig Little's arm and becomes overwhelmed with jealousy, then sadness and hurt.

"Don't get lost," Eddie says to Chrissy.

"No, don't let me come back and see some trick in your face," Chrissy replies and kisses Eddie on the cheek.

"Go on now wit' that craziness, woman," Eddie says with a grin.

Symoné sees Chrissy making her way through the crowded V.I.P. lounge and waves. Chrissy finally reaches Symoné and they hug.

"Chrissy, this is Craig. Craig Little, this is my best friend, Chrissy."

"Hi Chrissy, heard a lot about you."

"I hope nothing but good things," Chrissy says and laughs.

"Baby, Chrissy and I are going to play catch-up. I'll be back."

"Okay, if you need me, you know where I'm at," Craig Little says, reaching in his pocket, handing Symoné a G. She kisses him on the lips, puts the thousand dollars in her clutch, and walks out the V.I.P. area with Chrissy onto the crowded dance floor.

Mike keeps his eyes on Symoné and Chrissy and decides to follow them.

"Eddie, I'll be back. I want to talk with Symoné."

As Mike leaves, Craig Little approaches. "Sup Nice and Baby Nice?" Craig Little and Eddie show each other some love. "I hear Baby Nice doing his thing over at UNC."

"Yeah, took them to the championship," Eddie responds.

"Congrats, man," Craig Little says to Mike and embraces him.

"Thanks Little," Mike says. "I'm calling it a night ya'll. I'm out." He hugs his brother, tells the guys bye, and leaves the V.I.P. lounge. Eddie excuses himself and follows his brother. He puts his brother in a playful chokehold.

"I saw Little come in with Symoné. You all right, Mike?"

"Yeah, I'm good."

"If you say so. Just wanted to make sure." Eddie lets his brother out of the chokehold and goes back to enjoy the party in the V.I.P. area. Mike searches for Symoné.

✳ ✳ ✳

Symoné and Chrissy are at the bar, having a drink and talking. Symoné and Chrissy are so busy talking that they don't notice Mike.

"Can I have a bottle of your best champagne for the ladies?" Mike asks.

"Coming right up," the bartender says.

Symoné recognizes the voice, turns, and sees Mike standing behind her and Chrissy. Symoné is happy to see him. She gives him a hug and kiss on the cheek.

"Chrissy told me you were here. It's been a minute, Mike. How you been?"

"All right. How's Mykia?"

"She's good."

Mike leans on the bar, getting closer to Symoné.

Chrissy excuses herself, "I'll see you back in the V.I.P. lounge, Symoné," then walks off, leaving Symoné and Mike at the bar.

"Is everything all right? I cant seem to reach you, these days."

"Everything is much better now, and I'm seeing someone."

"Yeah, saw you coming in with him. Is it serious?"

"Yes, Mike it is. He's a good guy and treats Mykia and I well."

"What happened to us?"

Symoné gently places her hand on top of Mike's hand and looks into his eyes.

"I was dealing with a lot of stuff; the death of my father, the unexpected pregnancy, and I didn't want to bring you down with my problems."

"Bring me down? Never that. Your problems were my problems, and we were supposed to deal with them together."

"Certain things people just have to deal with alone and nobody can help," Symoné explains, staring into the distance for a brief moment. A tear falls down her face. Mike looks into her eyes and wipes the tear. "I didn't want to be a distraction for you, Mike; not with college and not with your promising basketball career ahead of you."

Mike interrupts, "Symoné, I really would like to spend some time with you and Mykia this summer, before I go back to school in August. You think you can make that happen?"

Symoné nods her head yes.

❋ ❋ ❋

Craig Little glances toward the dance floor from the V.I.P. lounge and notices Symoné and Mike looking very cozy. With a curious look on his face, Craig Little excuses himself from the conversation taking place among a group of guys. He makes his way through the crowded dance floor to the bar. Quincy stops him.

"Sup Little, can I holla at you a minute?" Quincy asks. Craig Little and Quincy walk away to a quieter area.

"What up?"

"That girl you came to the party with . . ."

"What about her?"

Quincy points out T-Bone in the crowd, dancing with some girl. "That nigga, T-Bone was talking some crazy shit and said he got a tape on her."

"Good lookin' out," Craig Little says, and then reaches into his pocket and slaps a knot of undisclosed an amount of money in his hand, as he embraces him. "Come through the block next week and let's talk." Craig Little turns from the direction of the bar and walks over to T-Bone.

Craig Little approaches T-Bone from behind.

"Hey Little," says the girl who's dancing with T-Bone.

T-Bone turns around and sees Craig Little with a serious look on his face.

"I heard you have a tape."

"Nah, what you talking 'bout, Little?"

Craig Little pulls up his shirt and puts his hand on his 9 mm. The girl backs out of the confrontation. "I'll talk to you later, T-Bone," she says, hurrying off the dance floor.

"We can do this the hard way or the easy way, homie. It's on you."

T-Bone holds his hands up. "You got it, Little. It's not that serious, my man, it's not that serious."

❀ ❀ ❀

Symoné looks out on the dance floor and sees T-Bone holding his hands up and Craig Little talking with him. She kisses Mike on the cheek. "Mike, I have to get back to my friend before he starts missing me. I promise I will give you a call."

Mike sits at the bar and watches Symoné with a slight smile on his face as she disappears in the crowd.

❀ ❀ ❀

"It is that serious to me, homie. So what I need you to do is meet me tomorrow at Wilson's, on one-five-eight, with the tape, around six."

"You got it, Little."

"And whatever happened between you and Symoné in the past, I need you to do me a favor and leave it there."

"No problem," T-Bone promises and walks off.

Symoné approaches as T-Bone is leaving. "Is everything okay? I saw you talking to T-Bone."

"Everything is all good. I saw you over at the bar talking with Mike Nice, all close. What's up with that?"

"That's my high school sweetheart, the guy I told you about."

"Mykia's father?"

Symoné nods her head yes.

"Small world. He's a good dude."

"Yeah, he is. Now let's talk about how good you are to me." Symoné puts her arms around Craig Little and gives him a big hug and kiss.

FAMILY BUSINESS

· ·

CHAPTER 12

It's late in the afternoon. Mae is sitting in front of her vanity, covering up the bruises on her face and neck with make-up. Baby Mykia is content, swaying back and forth to the lullaby coming from the small speaker attached to her baby swing.

Symoné walks into Mae's bedroom, "Hey Mom."

Mae is startled and drops her make-up powder brush.

"Sorry, didn't mean to startle you." Symoné walks in and takes Mykia out of the swing and gives her a big hug and kiss, then walks over to her mother.

Mae looks away to avoid eye contact with Symoné and to try and hide the bruises. "I forgot you still had keys. Jack just left for the store, and I wasn't expecting him back so soon."

Symoné leans over, looking into the mirror and gives her mother a hug and kiss. She notices the bruise on her mother's neck. She sits up and leans on the vanity. "You okay?"

"Yes, I'm fine, just a little tired. I need a vacation."

"What happened to your neck?"

"We had to restrain a patient that came in all high-up on the angel dust." Mae quickly changes the subject. "So, are you here to steal my grandbaby away?"

"Steal? Mom, you have Mykia all the time. You forget she's my baby," she says jokingly. "I have someone for you to meet downstairs."

"I finally get to meet this mystery man that has you and my grandbaby all the way out in Ridgewood, New Jersey? I was wondering when I was going to meet the guy."

"Well, he's downstairs in the living room."

"So what about Mike? You're not going to try and work that out for your daughter's sake?"

"I saw him last night. We talked and I think it's best we just stay friends."

"I think you're making a mistake."

"Maybe I am, but it's mine to make. Please come on down and meet my friend, Craig. I think you'll like him," Symoné says and leaves the bedroom with Mykia. Mae follows.

❋   ❋   ❋

Symoné and Mae walk down the stairs toward the living room. Craig Little is sitting on the sofa with flowers in his hand and several shopping bags. He stands when he sees the ladies coming down the stairs. Symoné introduces Mae to Craig Little.

"Mom, this is Craig Little and this is my mom, Mrs. Mae Harris."

Craig Little hands Mae the flowers. "Hello Mrs. Harris."

"You can call me Ms. Mae." Mae takes the flowers and puts them in a vase. They all sit on the sofa to talk, while Symoné bounces Mykia on her leg.

The front door opens and Jack enters with several grocery bags. Mae gets up from the sofa and hurries to take the groceries from Jack.

Symoné and Craig Little look at Mae oddly, observing how jumpy and overly attentive she is toward Jack.

Craig Little recognizes Jack. "I know your pops from somewhere," Craig Little whispers to Symoné.

"That's not my father. My father was killed."

"Wow, I'm sorry to hear that."

"Jack was my father's Partner."

"Partners," Craig Little repeats slowly, with a curious look on his face.

"Yeah, my pops and Jack were on some undercover sting over a year ago, in the Dunbar's, and they say my pops was killed in the line of duty." Symoné's mood changes and a tear fall from her eyes.

"I didn't mean to upset you, baby." Craig Little wipes the tear from her cheek and puts his arm around her.

"It's okay, you didn't know."

Craig Little's mind drifts for a moment to the night at the Dunbar, the night his solider, Caz was killed and framed by Detective Jack Fisher for Symoné's father's murder.

"I'm not trying to spoil your day talking about sad stuff. Let's head over to my mom's. She's waiting to meet you." Craig Little and Symoné get up off the sofa.

Mae puts the groceries on the kitchen counter and comes out with an open beer, handing it to Jack. Jack sits on the recliner next to the sofa.

"Jack, this is Craig. Symoné's friend. She brought him by for us to meet."

"How's it going?" Detective Fisher asks.

"It's all good," Craig Little replies.

"Symoné, leaving so soon? Where you been? You haven't been around in a while," Detective Fisher says.

"I've been busy, Jack," Symoné coldly responds without looking in his direction. "Mom, we have to go, Craig's mother has dinner waiting for us."

"Okay. Nice meeting you, Craig. I hope to see you again soon."

Symoné kisses her mom on the cheek. Mae hugs and kisses Mykia. "Nana loves you."

❊ ❊ ❊

Delia Little's dining room is elegant. The table is set for a feast with fine linen, china, and silverware. Craig Little holds Mykia and puts on her bib, as he and Symoné take a seat at the table.

Craig Little looks to Symoné, "So, what's up with you and Jack? I got the feeling you really don't care for him."

"I don't. After my father died he just eased his way into our lives. My mother's too blind to see he's no good."

Craig Little's mother, Delia, enters the dining room. She is seated in a wheelchair, being pushed by a private nurse. Craig Little hands Mykia to Symoné and takes the wheelchair from the nurse. He kisses his mother on the cheek, pushes her to the head of the table, and sits. A maid brings the food in and places it on the table.

"Sorry I had you young folks waiting so long."

"It's okay," says Symoné.

"Symoné, this is my mom, Mrs. Delia George."

"Hello Mrs. George."

"That's a beautiful baby you have there. She's so tiny."

"Yes, she is and so spoiled."

"So, you're Symoné. The young lady that stole my boy's heart."

Symoné blushes. "I did?"

"The last girl that stole my son's heart was a little girl back in kindergarten. What was that child's name, Craig?"

"I don't remember, ma."

"Jennifer. That's the child's name, Jennifer. That Jennifer had my baby sick. He couldn't eat for a week, because she didn't want to be his friend. He was in love with that Jennifer."

"Ma, I don't remember that."

"I remember. You had me so worried. Not eating and moping around the house."

"Ma, could we please stop going down memory lane and just eat." Symoné laughs.

Delia and Symoné continue to get acquainted over dinner. An hour goes by, and Craig Little looks at his watch. "Ma, I have some business to take care of. I will leave you ladies to talk. I'll be back." He kisses Delia, gently touches Symoné and Mykia, and leaves.

❈ ❈ ❈

The sun is going down and there's a cool breeze. A derelict with a cup in his hand is asking for change in front of Wilson's Restaurant, on the corner of West 158th Street and Amsterdam Avenue. Craig Little is talking on his mobile phone. He stops and puts a few dollars in the derelict's cup before going inside Wilson's.

A Ford Bronco with Maryland plates and tinted windows is double parked in front of Wilson's. The passenger side window slowly comes down, stopping halfway. Eyes peer out from underneath a baseball cap, watching

Craig Little walk into Wilson's. The window goes back up. A man dressed in an oversized black sweat suit gets out and scopes the area, before looking into Wilson's window storefront. He presses his face against the glass, cupping his hands to block the glare of the setting sun. He turns toward the Bronco and smiles', showing his top and bottom gold grills. He causally walks back to the Bronco, opens the front passenger door, and gets in. Moments later the back door to the Bronco opens and T-Bone gets out with a VHS tape in his hand.

❋   ❋   ❋

When T-Bone walks over to the table, Willow and Dobie are finishing their dinner.

"Sup Little?"

"You tell me."

T-Bone hands Craig Little the tape. Craig Little hands the tape to Dobie. "Do me a favor. Go in the bathroom with him, and make sure he pulls all the ribbon out of the tape and burns it."

Dobie walks with T-Bone to the bathroom, and a few minutes later they come out without the tape.

"We good, Little?"

Craig Little nods his head yes and T-Bone leaves.

❋   ❋   ❋

The Bronco is still double parked out front. Craig Little, Willow, and Dobie exit the restaurant. Willow notices the Bronco. "That Bronco been double parked outside for a minute."

Craig Little looks over at the Bronco, and then looks down at his beeping pager. It's Symoné. He calls her on his mobile phone. "Hey baby, I'm on my way back to the house now. Hold on a minute." Craig Little gives Willow and Dobie a pound. "I'll holla at ya'll later." He continues talking with Symoné, as he walks to his Benz that is parked on the corner across the street from Wilson's. Willow and Dobie walk in the opposite direction.

Willow looks back and notices the Bronco start up and move slowly in Craig Little's direction. Willow puts his hand on his 9mm under his shirt. "Yo Dobie, heads up. It looks like that Bronco's followin' Little."

Dobie pulls his 9mm out, puts it down by his side, and they quickly follow the Bronco on foot. Willow comes up on the passenger side and Dobie on the driver's side.

The windows on the passenger side of the Bronco come down slightly. Willow's eyes widen when he see the barrels of guns pointing out the windows in Craig Little's direction. "LITTLE, IT'S A HIT!" He pulls his 9mm and fires on the Bronco, and Dobie fires his gun at the driver's side.

Still on the phone, Craig Little turns toward the sound of Willow's voice and gunfire, a confused look on his face. He sees Willow and Dobie firing. He drops the mobile, pulls his 9mm, and starts firing at the Bronco. People are screaming, ducking down, and running for cover. Gunfire is coming from the Bronco's window and shatters Wilson's glass storefront, hitting the derelict. The man falls to the ground, dead. Craig Little is grazed by a bullet on the arm. He takes cover and aims his gun at the Bronco's tires and shoots. The Bronco spins out of control, hitting parked cars, then comes to an abrupt stop. The riddled door opens, full of bullet holes, and T-Bone's bloody body, with his gun still in hand, falls out on the ground, dead. The man in the oversized black sweat suit and two other hit men, battered and bloody, stumble out of the Bronco, still firing their automatics.

Willow and Dobie have taken cover behind the parked cars along Amsterdam. They fire upon the hit men killing them all. Then they run over to check on Craig Little. They see the blood coming from his shoulder.

"You hit, we gonna get you to the hospital, Little," Willow says.

"I'm good. The bullet just grazed me," Craig Little explains. Police sirens can be heard in the distance. "Five-o will be here any minute. I'll hit ya'll up later."

They hurry to their cars and leave the bloody scene.

❋ ❋ ❋

Symoné is in the family room with Delia, eating sweet potato pie, and listening to jazz. Mykia is asleep on a cashmere blanket that rests on the thick, peach carpeted floor. There is a Baby Grand piano in the corner of the room, covered with many family photos. Pictures of famous jazz musicians cover the wall. The private nurse enters the family room, with a glass of water and several pills on a tray.

"It's time for your medicine, Mrs. Little."

"I'm so tired of all these pills," Delia says, her hand shaking as she takes her medication.

"I am so glad Craig finally found someone. He thinks I'ma live forever, but I'm getting older and weaker. He's my world and all I got. I'm old, but not senile, yet. He thinks I don't know what he's doing, but I do. Craig's father died when he was very young. He had a stroke right in front of him. My baby grew up so fast, determined to be the man of the house. He always brought home good grades. He was an honor roll student, got accepted by several top colleges, and got his degree from NYU Stern School of Business."

"Really? I didn't know that," Symoné replies, surprised. She nestles herself back in the soft, oversized couch to make better eye contact with Delia.

"He had a good job at Goldman Sachs, but left it for the streets and that fast money," Delia continues, with a noticeable change in her tone. "Yes, it helps pay the bills and affords us a lifestyle that most people dream of. But it's a dangerous business, child, and I'm afraid for him."

Moments later the private nurse enters back into the family room. "Ms. Delia, it's getting late and I need to get you ready for bed."

"Baby, you gonna be all right down here by yourself?"

"I'll be fine, Mrs. George."

"You can call me Mama Dee."

"Okay Mama Dee, goodnight."

Ms. Delia leaves the family room with her private nurse. Symoné gets up from the sofa, looking at all the photos and fiddling with the keys on the piano. She decides to explore the large house, when she suddenly finds Craig Little in a bathroom off by the kitchen area, cleaning blood off his arm.

She quickens her pace, reaching for his arm. "When did you get here and what happened to you?"

"Had a little situation, but everything is good now."

"Everything is good? There's blood all over your clothes, Craig!" Symoné reaches for the area on Craig's shirt where the bullet grazed him.

Craig takes the bloody shirt off, exposing his broad, muscled chest and washboard abs, while reaching for Symoné and pulling her close. He kisses her on the lips and she kisses him back.

She tries to pull away to continue attending to his arm. "Craig, I'm afraid."

He pulls her closer, notices her sad, but gorgeous and alluring brown-eyes for the first time and is mesmerized by her beauty. "You're beautiful Symoné?"

"Craig I'm being serious. I don't want to lose you."

"You're not going to lose me, Symoné." Craig tenderly cups her face with his warm hands and brings his soft lips to hers, giving her the most loving and passionate kiss. A chill goes through her body, goose bumps cover her arms.

Craig Little gently lifts Symoné up, putting her on the edge of the bathroom sink. They gaze at each other for a moment, then share a hungry kiss.

As Craig Little kisses Symoné, he can't help but notice her soft breasts pressed against his muscular chest. He can feel his member harden. In seconds they tear each other's clothes off.

Symoné runs her eyes greedily over his chiseled body and wraps her legs around his waist. She looks down at the fullness of his member and it arouses her even more.

Craig Little licks his lips as he gazes at her pert, round breasts. As he runs his thumbs over them, Symoné sighs. She pulls him closer; running her hands over the rippling muscles of his firm, smooth back. She feels an intense rush of heat and sensation at her core when she feels his member touch the lips of her womanhood. She moans, then reaches for his manhood and eases him inside her. He leans down and whispers into her ear, "I love you."

"I love you, too, Craig."

They heave against each other and he can feel the slick wetness of her excitement. He quickens his pace as Symoné's moans get louder and her legs start to tremble and shake uncontrollably. The strong, lovely sensation begins to claim her.

"Craig, I'm cumming," she cries out.

Craig Little's legs become weak and start to buckle from underneath him. He lifts Symoné, holding her close as her arms are wrapped around his neck. He sits on the closed toilet seat and holds her down by her shoulders to keep her firm on top of his manhood. He feels her core tighten around his shaft.

Symoné cums and her sweet lava flows onto Craig Little's inner thighs. He follows and abandons himself to pleasure.

WELCOME TO MY WORLD

. . . .

CHAPTER 13

Several weeks have passed since the unsuccessful hit on Craig Little.

Craig Little pulls his Benz into a deserted lot in New Jersey with Symoné, parks, reaches into the glove compartment, and takes out a clip and a .380 semi-automatic gun.

"I never touched a gun before, I'm kind of scared."

"Baby, never be scared of no gun. It may be the very thing that saves your life or mine. It's crazy out here, and I need to know that you can protect yourself."

Symoné and Craig Little get out of the car. He shows her how to load the clip and work the safety. She practices, while he looks for some empty cans and bottles. He stands them up, side by side, on an upside down garbage can in the corner of the lot.

"Symoné, give me the .380, so I can show you how it's done."

"Okay, Jesse James."

Craig Little takes the .380, aims with one hand, shoots, and hits one of the cans, knocking it over. He then stands behind Symoné. She rubs her rear against his manhood.

"Come on now, Symoné, this is serious. I need you to pay attention to what I'm doing. This is not a game."

Craig Little positions the gun in her hand and pulls the trigger, hitting another can. Symoné is startled by the sound and force of the .380. He releases her hand, so she can practice shooting on her own. She misses a few times, and then begins to hit the cans and bottles. He smiles proudly as he looks on at his student handling the .380.

"I think you are starting to enjoy yourself a little too much. Come on, let's get out of here."

Craig Little hears his mobile phone in the Benz. He hurries over and answers; it's Willow.

"Sup," Craig Little says.

"We need to get to Philly. DeWitt hit me up and said that nigga, Quincy trippin'. He was seen all up in the club acting like a baller and trickin' hard on some skeezers," Willow reports.

"Word?"

"I knew that nigga wasn't ready," Willow says.

"I need you to get two round trips on Amtrak to Philly. I'll head out first thing in the morning," Craig Little says.

"Everything okay?" asks Symoné.

"Yeah. Now let's go get something to eat."

❋ ❋ ❋

Craig Little and Symoné are at home in Ridgewood, New Jersey. He is sitting in his bedroom, counting stacks of money, and talking on the telephone with Willow. "I just got the call; we need to head out to Cali."

"What about Quincy?" Willow asks.

"I'll send Symoné to pick that up."

"Symoné to pick up what?" Symoné joins the conversation, as she walks into the bedroom in her nightgown, looking very exhausted. She pulls back the blankets and gets into bed.

"I'll see you tomorrow." Craig hangs up the telephone. "I see you finally got Mykia to go to sleep?"

"Yes, finally. That girl is a handful."

"I need you to do me a favor in the morning. I need to go to Cali."

"Cali? For how long?"

"Just a few days."

"Baby, when is the money you make going to be enough?"

"I'm almost there."

"I hope so. You're always running. It gets lonely when you're away."

Craig Little puts the money down and reaches over and gives Symoné a hug and kiss. "Give me a month or so, and I am done with all this running."

"That's what your mouth says. I have to see it to believe it. So, what you need me to do in the morning?"

"You think you can get a babysitter?"

"Yes."

"I need you to go to Philly and pick up some money."

"Okay," Symoné replies, and then goes to sleep.

Craig Little makes a call. "Sup Dob, need you in the morning."

❋ ❋ ❋

It's early the next day. The Amtrak train is crowded with people in business suits and briefcases. Symoné is in her seat asleep, with Mykia strapped to her in a baby carrier, and a baby bag in the seat next to her.

"Next stop, 30th Street Station, Philadelphia," the conductor announces.

Symoné wakes and exits the train.

Quincy has his homeboy, Nico, a stick-up kid, waiting at the station for Symoné. He is a stocky man in his early twenties, casually dressed in a sweat suit and sneakers. He's not bad looking, except for the scar on his face and side of his neck. Nico stands on the platform, looking at a picture of Symoné and then at the people exiting the train. He spots Symoné and hurries out the station.

Symoné exits the 30th Street Station and is feeding Mykia a bottle. She is stopped by Nico at the exit.

"Excuse me miss, do you know if that train just came in from New York?"

"Yes, I just got off that train."

"Thank you, miss."

Symoné continues on her way to the livery stand. She does not know that Craig Little has sent Dobie to watch her back. Dobie is sitting in a hooptie with Delaware plates, in the passenger drop-off area near the livery stand. He is dressed like a college frat boy, wearing a fraternity t-shirt with a matching hat. He has a Street Sweeper Semi-Automatic on the passenger seat, a pair of leather gloves, and a nine tucked in the waist of his jeans. He sees Symoné stop for a brief moment to talk with Nico and is surprised when he sees her with the baby.

Dobie directs his attention back to Nico. He studies him hard and notices the scars on his face and neck. He sees him hurry over to a payphone.

"Yeah, she here and got a baby with her." Nico hangs up the phone, hurries to his old Cadillac parked in a no standing zone, and gets in.

Symoné gets into a livery cab and it pulls off. Nico follows the cab in the Cadillac and Dobie follows the Cadillac, keeping his distance in the hooptie, making sure he does not lose sight of the cab.

❋ ❋ ❋

Quincy is in the living room, whispering in the receiver of the phone, and putting stacks of money into a sneaker box.

"Nah nigga . . . just get the money, and I'll meet ya back at the spot."

Symoné walks into the living room with Mykia on her hip, drying her hands with a paper towel. Quincy quickly hangs up the phone.

"It's getting late, Quincy. Do you have the money ready yet?"

"Yeah, it's ready."

"Good, please call me a cab."

"I'll take you to the station." Quincy puts the sneaker box into a shopping bag.

Symoné gets Mykia ready and they leave.

❋ ❋ ❋

Dobie is parked in the hooptie, watching Quincy's house on North Board Street. Quincy has the shopping bag full of money and exits the house with Symoné and Mykia. They get into the same Cadillac Dobie saw following Symoné from the Amtrak Station. Dobie pulls out of a parking space and follows the Cadillac back to the station.

Nico, Quincy's stick-up kid, is sitting outside the station on a bench, wearing an expensive suit. He pretends to read and hides his face with a newspaper. The Cadillac pulls up in the drop-off area. Quincy gets out with the shopping bag, opens the passenger door, and helps Symoné get out with Mykia.

Dobie pulls up in the hooptie and parks a few cars away from the Cadillac. He watches Symoné and Quincy go into the station. A few minutes later he sees Quincy exit the station without the shopping bag, stopping for a brief moment to talk with Nico, and then gets into his Cadillac.

Nico puts the newspaper down on the bench and goes into the station. Dobie watches and notices the scar on his face and neck, realizing it's the same man that was driving Quincy's Cadillac earlier that day. Dobie puts his car signal lights on, puts the Street Sweeper on the floor on the passenger side, gets out, and goes into the station.

❀　❀　❀

Symoné boards the train with Mykia, her baby bag, and now the shopping bag. She finds a seat, places the shopping bag on the floor between her feet, puts Mykia's baby bag on the seat next to her, and rests her head back.

Nico enters the car and sits in the empty seat behind Symoné. He leans forward and whispers into her ear. She twists her face and turns around.

"Excuse me?"

Nico gets up, stands directly in front of Symoné, revealing his gun tucked in the waist of his suit pants.

Symoné's eyes grow big. "Please, don't hurt us."

"Just be cool and give me the money."

Symoné hands Nico the shopping bag and he calmly walks down the aisle to the exit, right past the conductor collecting tickets.

"Ticket, sir."

"Nah, I was just saying bye to a friend."

"Hurry off, sir; we're getting ready to pull out," the conductor says to Nico. "Tickets, please, everyone please have your tickets out."

The conductor approaches Symoné.

"Ticket, miss."

Symoné's hands are shaking as she searches for her ticket in the baby bag.

"Are you all right, miss?"

"Yes," Symoné lies. She hands her ticket to the conductor. The conductor continues down the aisle, collecting tickets as the train slowly moves out of the station. Symoné stares out the window with a blank look on her face.

"Next Station, Wilmington, Delaware."

❋ ❋ ❋

Dobie is standing at the newsstand in the station, buying a magazine, when Nico comes down the escalator with the shopping bag. He watches him walk toward the exit. He follows him and sees him put the shopping bag in the back seat of the Cadillac, then Quincy pulls off with Nico on the passenger side.

Dobie hurries to the hooptie, heads toward the North 30th Street Station and catches them at the light on Market Street. The Cadillac pulls off when the light turns green and Dobie follows at a distance. Quincy rides down Market Street for a while to make sure no one is following him. He gets on the highway for several exits, makes several twists and turns, and ends up back at his house on North Board Street. Quincy parks the Cadillac.

Dobie pulls up alongside Quincy and beeps his horn. Quincy rolls down his window. Dobie, with his finger on the Street Sweeper trigger, leans over to the passenger side.

"Excuse me, I'm lost. Can you tell me how to get to Fairmount Park?"

"You a long way off, frat boy," retorts Nico.

Quincy, with his hand still on the steering wheel, sticks his head and hand out of the window, ready to give Dobie directions, when Dobie raises the Street Sweeper, points it at the side of Quincy's head, and shoots. Nico freezes. Several bullets hit Quincy in the upper torso and head, taking off part of his skull, splattering his brain all over the dashboard and window. He slumps dead on top of Nico, who is hit but still alive.

Dobie puts the Street Sweeper back down on the passenger seat, puts on his leather gloves, gets out the hooptie, and walks over to Nico in the Cadillac. He opens the passenger door and Nico's body falls halfway out onto the ground, along with the broken glass from the window. His clothes are soaked in blood and some of Quincy's brain matter. His eyes are rolling back in his head. He is gurgling and spitting up blood. Dobie stands over him, pulls the 9mm tucked in the waist of his jeans, and shoots him twice in the head, killing him. He opens the back door and takes out the shopping bag with the money, gets back into the hooptie, and pulls off.

❋ ❋ ❋

Symoné and Mykia are home in New Jersey, safe and sound on the sofa, still with their clothes on from the trip to Philly. All the lights are turned on in the house. Mykia is asleep on the mink throw rug in the living room. Symoné sits on the sofa nodding off, fighting to keep her eyes open.

The telephone rings. Symoné jumps up, extremely nervous. She hurries, tripping over the furniture to get to the telephone hanging on the wall in the kitchen.

"Hello?"

"Hey baby."

"I've been trying to reach you all evening."

"I know."

"I left several messages for you at the front desk of the hotel."

"I know. I'm just getting in. Are you and Mykia okay?"

"Craig, I need to talk to you."

"I know, it's okay."

"No, you don't understand, they took the money. I got robbed."

"It's okay, I know."

"You know?"

"Yeah, we got the money back. Everything is okay."

"How? I'm confused."

"Just know I handled it and got the money back."

"Thank God, I was going crazy."

"Why'd you take Mykia with you?"

"I called my mother to watch Mykia. She wasn't feeling well, and Chrissy was in Jamaica with her man. I couldn't reach you and I didn't know what to do, so I took her with me. I didn't think I'd be robbed."

"That's my fault. I should have never sent you. I'm glad ya'll okay. I finished up my business here early. I'll be home tomorrow."

"Good."

"Love you."

"Love you, too," Symoné says and hangs up the phone. She takes a deep breath and smiles.

END OF THE ROAD, JACK

. . . .

CHAPTER 14

Summertime, June 1990

It's been almost two years since Mae's husband murder. She has on a washed out lounge dress and her once radiant smile and attractive looks are fading away. She has gained weight, her eyes are dark and puffy, and she looks very tired. She is dusting the furniture and tidying up the house, when the doorbell rings. She opens the door and it is Internal Affairs Investigators, Bobby Washington and Dennis Jones. Washington and Jones show their badges, Mae lets them in, and they have a seat.

"Would you gentlemen care for some water or juice?"

"No, thank you," Jones and Washington respond.

"First, we would like to extend our condolences to you for the loss of your husband," Jones says.

"Thank you."

"We are here, because we received an anonymous tip that Detective Fisher may have killed your husband and planted the murder weapon on the perp, who was also killed at the crime scene," Jones explains.

"No," Mae says and shakes her head in disbelief. "No, I don't believe it. Jack and my husband had been friends since childhood and did everything together, school, the police academy."

"Are you aware that Detective Fisher is under investigation for police corruption?" Washington reveals.

"Police corruption?"

"Yes," Jones confirms.

"I don't know what to say right now, I'm speechless."

The front door opens and it's Detective Jack Fisher. He comes into the house and slams the door behind him. "What the hell are you doing here?"

Washington and Jones have a look of surprise on their faces when they see Detective Fisher use his own keys to come into the house.

"We didn't know you lived here," Washington says.

"I don't. I just come from time to time to check on Mae and see if she needs anything."

Mae looks at Fisher is confused by his response to the Investigators about their living arrangement.

"Well Mrs. Harris, we're going to leave now," Jones says.

"Yes, but if you have anything that may help our investigation, please do not hesitate to give us a call," Washington adds, handing Mae a business card.

Detective Fisher opens the front door and Washington and Jones leave. Detective Fisher peeks out of the living room window from behind the curtain, watching Washington and Jones get into their car and pull off.

"Jack, what's going on and why did you lie to the investigators about you living here?"

"Nothing is going on and I don't want people all up in my business at the precinct."

"Jack, what happen the night my husband died?"

"What you mean? What did they tell you?"

"A whole lot. I need to know the truth right here and right now. Did you have anything to do with my husband's death?"

"What? Are you crazy? Is that what they told you? They get paid to tell lies and bring down good officers. What other lies did they tell you about me?"

"Why didn't you tell me you were under investigation?"

"I didn't want to worry you."

"Worry me? You didn't think I needed to know that, and then you tell them you just drop in to check on me? I don't even know who you are anymore, Jack, all the lies and deceit. I'm done."

"What you mean, you done?"

"I'm done, Jack. I need you to gather your things and leave tonight."

The telephone rings. Mae goes into the kitchen and picks up the phone. "Hello?"

"Hey mom, I need you to babysit for me tonight. Craig has some surprise planned for me."

"Not tonight."

Fisher is talking in the background, "What you mean, you done? You let them get all up in your head . . . Now you talking crazy!"

"What's going on?" asks Symoné.

"Jack, I'm on the phone," Mae yells.

"We need to talk, now!" Fisher demands, then takes the phone out of Mae's hand and hangs it up.

❊ ❊ ❊

Symoné sits on the edge of the bed, looking perplexed at the receiver in her hand. Craig Little walks into the room.

"We're going to have to cancel tonight."

"What's wrong?"

"I'm not sure; my mother sounded funny on the phone. Jack was yelling at her in the background and the next thing I know, the phone went dead. I need to get to the house."

"Okay, call your girl Chrissy and see if she'll watch Mykia and then we'll head over to your mother's house," Craig says, getting his nine out of the closet and tucking it into the waist of his pants.

❊ ❊ ❊

"Why would you hang up the telephone on my daughter? What's wrong with you? I'm tired of you. I'm tired of the lies, tired of the abuse. I want you out of my house, now," Mae exclaims and turns to walk away.

Fisher grabs Mae's arm tight. She tries to pull away, but his grip is too strong. She scratches the side of his face, causing the skin to break. He lets go of her arm, touches his face, and feels the blood streaming.

"You fucking bitch," Fisher says. Then, with all his strength, he hits Mae with a backhanded slap to the face, causing her to fall backward onto the glass picture frames hanging on the wall, shattering them.

Mae is in pain. Holding her face, she struggles to get up from the floor. Fisher is enraged and grabs her off the floor and tosses her like a rag doll onto the coffee table, breaking it. She is bloody and bruised, but is able to lift herself up, reach for the lamp off the end table, and hit him in the head. It does not faze him and only makes him angrier. He kneels over her broken body, removes his .38-caliber revolver from his shoulder holster, and puts it on the end table by the sofa. Then he proceeds to choke her and rip open her lounge dress. She spits in his face, trying to fight back and pry his hand from her neck, but he is too strong. She gasps for air and then passes out.

❋ ❋ ❋

Craig Little and Symoné pull up and park the Benz in front of Mae's house. All appears calm and quiet. Craig Little opens the door and gets out. Symoné sits for a moment, looks into the rearview mirror, and reflects back to the night she was raped by Detective Jack Fisher.

Symoné remembers: The weight of Jack's wet, sweaty body on top of hers, gagging from his sweat dripping into her mouth, the pain he inflicted on her.

Symoné takes a deep breath, opens the glove compartment, and takes out the .380 Criag Little bought her, putting it in her handbag.

"What you need that for?"

"I've been having this nervous feeling in my stomach, since we left the house."

"You know you can't pull a gun out on somebody and not use it? You ready for that?"

"I don't know," Symoné admits, getting out the Benz. They proceed down the curved, stone walkway to the house.

Symoné uses her key to open the door. She finds the living room in disarray, Mae unconscious and bloody, her breasts exposed and lounge dress torn open, and Fisher on top of her lifeless body, raping her.

"What the fuck!" Craig Little exclaims, pulling his 9mm from his waist and pointing it at Fisher. "Get the fuck up, nigga," he demands, cautiously approaching Fisher.

Fisher turns and sees the nine pointed at him and tries to reach for his .38 on the end table. Craig Little shoots a warning shot, hitting the end table.

"Don't try it, muthafucker."

Fisher slowly gets up. Craig Little becomes impatient and kicks him hard, knocking him off Mae, onto the floor. Fisher sits up and leans his back against the sofa.

"So, what are you going to do? Shoot a cop?"

Symoné kneels down beside Mae, checks to see if she is alive and breathing, and then fixes her mother's clothes. Mae is starting to move around and wakes from her unconscious state.

"What you wanna do, Symoné?" asks Craig Little.

Symoné sees Fisher's .38 on the end table and picks it up. She cocks it back and points it at Fisher. She looks terrified and her hands are shaking.

"You're going to let a girl do your dirt for you?"

Craig Little hits Fisher in the head with the butt of his nine, opening his forehead. Fisher grabs his head and is in a great deal of pain.

"Now, shut the fuck up, nigga, before I shoot you. You owe anyway."

Fisher and Symoné look at Craig Little, puzzled.

"Yeah, nigga. I saw what you did. I was in the Dunbar that night. I saw you put the bullet in that cop."

"What?" Symoné steadies her aim.

"Yeah, your father caught him stealing drug money and he killed him, and then planted the gun on my boy, Caz."

"Jack, you killed my father?" Symoné asks as tears fall from her eyes.

"He is lying to you, Symoné. Why would I kill your father?"

Symoné looks at her mother, lying on the floor helpless, and then back at Fisher. "You destroyed our lives, took everything from us." She closes her eyes and pulls the trigger, hitting Fisher in the middle of the forehead, killing him instantly with his own .38 revolver.

❀ ❀ ❀

The quiet suburb area is now a crime scene. There are several patrol cars, a black coroner's van, and an ambulance with flashing lights, parked in the front of the two-story, red brick house. An officer is putting yellow tape up, while other officers in uniforms and suits, wearing gloves, are going in and out of the house. EMT brings Mae out on a stretcher and lifts her into the ambulance. Two female officers are bringing out Symoné in handcuffs. She has a dazed look on her face. Craig Little walks beside her to the patrol car.

"It's going to be okay. Remember what I said. Do not say anything else to the cops until you have a lawyer. I'll see you at the precinct."

Symoné looks at Craig Little and nods her head. The officers put her into the patrol car and pull off.

Symoné sits quietly in a small interrogation room. Her heart-shaped locket is open, and she stares at the picture of her and her father. She starts to cry and wipes away her tears with the soiled, crumbled-up tissue in her hand.

The door opens. Symoné quickly closes the locket, gains her composure, and sits up straight. Internal Affairs Investigators, Washington and Jones, enter the room. Jones places a box of Kleenex tissue on the table. They take a seat.

"Hello Symoné. How are you doing?" asks Jones.

"Okay, I guess."

"We've been to the hospital and your mother sustained some extensive injuries," Washington shares.

"Symoné, can you tell us what happened?" asks Jones.

"Is she going to be all right?"

"She was beat up pretty badly; a broken jaw, ribs. Her eyes are black and swollen. She can barely open them, but she's going to be okay with time," Washington confirms.

Symoné buries her head in her arms and cries.

"Symoné, can you tell us what happen?" Jones repeats.

"Did you shoot Detective Fisher with his gun?" Washington asks.

"We can't help you if you don't tell us something," Jones says.

Symoné lifts her head and her eyes are blood-shot from crying. She takes a tissue and wipes her face.

"We came by and spoke to your mother earlier today. Did she tell you that?" asks Washington.

Symoné shakes her head no.

"Detective Fisher was a corrupt cop," Washington continues.

Symoné, with puffy, red-eyes, looks directly at Washington, and listens closely as he speaks.

"We believe Detective Fisher may have murdered your father and covered it up," Washington shares.

"It would be considered justifiable homicide if you were protecting yourself and your mother," Jones explains.

The tears fall down Symoné's face, and she cries uncontrollably as she hangs her head down.

"I was pro . . . tecting us," Symoné sniffles through her tears, "Y...yes, I did it . . . I shot him . . . I shot Jack . . . He hurt me . . . He hurt my mother . . . I pulled the trigger."

The door to the interrogation room flies open. A well-dressed, distinguished looking African American man in a bow tie enters the room.

"I'm Tony Ricco, attorney for Symoné Harris, and your interrogation of my client is over." Ricco hands them a business card. "If you need to speak with my client again, please give my office a call." Ricco helps Symoné up from the chair and they leave Washington and Jones sitting in the interrogation room alone.

"I guess our investigation on Detective Jack Fisher is closed, huh," Jones says.

"I'd say so. We can't investigate a dead man, can we," Washington says.

"Justice served," Jones says.

"On a platter," Washington finishes.

Washington and Jones get up and leave the interrogation room with satisfied looks on their faces.

NOTHING LASTS FOREVER

· ·

CHAPTER 15

Two months after Detective Jack Fisher's murder, Symoné is having nightmares, tossing and turning in her sleep.

Jack is drunk and laughing, as Symoné stands in front of him, trembling and pointing a .380 semi-automatic.

"If you shoot me, then Mykia will be fatherless . . . Another bastard child . . . growing up in the ghetto without a father."

"Mike is Mykia's father."

"How you know?"

"Cause I know."

"You sure, cause Mykia looks a lot like me."

Symoné looks over at the playpen and sees Mike Blackwell take Mykia out. "Do you even know who the father is?" asks Mike, laughing uncontrollably.

Jack grabs the .380 out of Symoné's hand and slaps her across the face with it, knocking her onto the sofa, unconscious. Symoné wakes and finds Jack on top of her without a shirt and his pants unzipped. Jack leans over to kiss Symoné and she bites his lip and spits in his face. Jack becomes enraged and puts his hands around Symoné's neck and chokes her. Symoné gasps for air and tries to pry Jack's hands from around her neck. Symoné sees the .380 automatic on the coffee table beside the sofa, she grabs it and shoots.

Symoné wakes suddenly; disoriented and frightened. She looks over at Craig Little and he is knocked out cold. She hears Mykia's cries coming from across the hall. She hurries out of the bed and into Mykia's bedroom.

Mykia's bedroom is painted in pastel colors, with painted butterflies on the ceiling. The room is packed with all the things a little baby would need and want. Symoné enters the bedroom and takes Mykia out of her crib. Mykia stops crying, and she sits with the baby in the rocking chair. Mykia looks up at Symoné with her big, bright brown eyes, which makes Symoné smile, and then her eyes fill with tears and sadness. She closes her eyes, rocks back and forth with Mykia in her arms, and a tear falls from her eye onto Mykia's cheek.

❋ ❋ ❋

It's early afternoon. Symoné sits on the sofa with a t-shirt and shorts on, changing Mykia's diaper, when the doorbell rings. She has a surprised look on her face and gets up with Mykia and opens the door to find Chrissy on her front porch.

"Chrissy? What are you doing here?"

"Are you going to invite me in or are we going to have a conversation out here on the porch?"

"Come in, crazy lady. How did you find us way out here in Jersey?"

Chrissy comes in, takes Mykia from Symoné, kisses her, and they sit on the sofa to talk.

"I called your mother. Where you been hiding, girl?"

"Here, just taking care of Mykia."

"Where's Craig?"

"He left early this morning to take care of some business."

"Well come on, get dressed. It's the championship game at the Rucker."

"I don't know, girl. I really don't want to see Mike right now. I know he's mad at me since I haven't brought Mykia down to the city to see him."

"Why?"

"I've been really caught up and have a lot going on."

"What does that have to do with him seeing his daughter?"

"I just . . ."

"Whatever happened with you and Mike? He was always so good to you."

"Yeah, he was. I just wasn't ready."

"You think you two will ever get back together?"

"Nah, too much has happened, and I love Craig, now. He's good to me and Mykia."

"I hear you, but that should not stop you from allowing Mike to see and spend time with his daughter."

"I promise you, I'll make sure, Mike see her before he goes back to school."

"Good, now get something on before we miss the game."

❋ ❋ ❋

The sun is beaming down, the weather is humid, and the temperature has reached over ninety-five degrees; a record-breaking number. The DJ in the Rucker's Park is blasting Rob Base & DJ E-Z Rock's, "Joy and Pain". Lines of people are on W. 155th Street, around the park, and down the block, trying to make their way into the basketball court to get a seat for the Rucker's basketball championship game.

Despite the heat, everyone is out enjoying the day. The strong aroma from the frankfurter carts and food vendors fill the air. Old men are sitting in the park, playing chess in the shade. Children are playing on the swings and monkey bars, while other children wait patiently on line with their parents at the icy-man cart and Good Humor truck. The fire hydrants are on full blast; dogs and children play in the water, trying to cool off from the heat. Many young women sporting fresh manicures, pedicures, and hairdos are standing around, half-dressed, showing off their best assets, trying to pick up guys. The guys with their fresh haircuts are laced in expensive jewelry, showing off their motorcycles and flashy cars.

Chrissy pulls up with Symoné in a convertible BMW. They get out and walk toward the park. Mike and Georgie, are standing at the icy-cart waiting, when he sees Symoné.

"Georgie, I'll meet you on the court. I need to holla at Symoné a minute."

Mike gets off the line and jogs over to Symoné and Chrissy, catching them before they go into the basketball court.

"Hey. Sup?"

"Hey Mike. Where's Eddie, is he here yet?" asks Chrissy.

"He should be here shortly. Hello Symoné."

"Hey Mike."

"Symoné, I'ma give you two some privacy. I'll be waiting for you at the gate entrance." Chrissy walks off.

"So, what's going on? I haven't heard from you since the Jerry Wells party. I even went to your mother's house several times, but no one answered the door."

"My mother's in the hospital."

"Is everything okay?"

"Yeah, she's going to be fine."

"That's good. So, you still with Little?"

"Yeah, we're living out in Jersey."

"Wow, that was fast."

"What you mean by that?"

"I'm just saying, his lifestyle, why would you want Mykia around all that."

"How can you judge a man that you don't even know?"

"He's a drug dealer."

"And, what that have to do with how he treats me and Mykia? By the way, in case you forgot, your brother, Eddie doesn't work a 9 to 5 either."

"Don't change the subject, Symoné. I thought you were smarter than that."

"Okay Mike, this conversation is over. I'll speak with you later."

Symoné attempts to walk away. Mike grabs her arm. Chrissy notices the confrontation and all the people starting to gather around the couple, and hurries over.

"Okay, I'm sorry, Symoné. I'm just trying to talk you."

"Now is not a good time, Mike."

"When is it ever a good time, Symoné?"

"Mike, let's talk about this later." Symoné attempts to walk away again and Mike blocks her with his body, forcing her back onto the park fence.

"No, I want to talk to you now!"

"Mike, you have a game. That's where your focus and concern should be right now."

"Fuck that."

Chrissy reaches the gate. "Okay everybody, the show is over." The people start to disperse.

"What's going on, you two?"

"Your girlfriend is trippin'."

"Nah, you the one really trippin'."

Craig Little and Willow happen to be walking up the block toward the Rucker's Park. They see in Symoné's face and her up against the fence. Craig Little and Willow hurry over.

"Sup Mike?" asks Craig Little.

Symoné turns to the sound of Craig Little's voice and is surprised to see him and Willow.

"Sup?" Mike says to Craig Little.

"I see you got my girl all up against the fence. What's going on?"

"Come on, baby, let's go," Symoné says to Craig Little.

"No, Symoné. I'm just asking the brother a question."

"This doesn't concern you, Little," says Mike.

"I think it does. Symoné is with me now and no longer your concern, my man."

"Symoné is always going to be my concern, brother, and Mykia, too."

Mike and Craig Little are in each other's face, going back and forth arguing, and getting loud. The crowd is starting to gather around again.

Chrissy takes Mike's hand and tries to lure him away from the argument with Craig Little. "Mike, let's go, the game is about to start," she says.

Mike tunes Chrissy out and continues arguing with Craig Little.

Symoné stands between them and tries to stop the argument.

"Mike, you making a scene and people are starting to stare."

"I don't care. Fuck these people." Mike pushes Symoné out of the way, and she stumbles back into Chrissy.

Craig Little hits Mike with a right hook to the jaw, stunning him. Mike comes back with a left hook and then a right, making Craig Little stagger.

Symoné and Chrissy are screaming for them to stop fighting and attempt to intervene. But Willow holds them back and keeps them out of harms ways.

Craig Little charges Mike like a bull, hitting him with thunderous blows to the sides and kidney region, and lands some vicious shots to the head. Mike Blackwell hits Craig Little with a hard left hook that brings his head to an upward position and quickly follows with a hard right straight to the face. The blows cause Craig Little to stumble to the ground, exposing his 9mm tucked in his pant waist. Mike rushes Craig Little, while he is on the ground, and reaches for the nine. Craig Little pulls the 9mm from his waist, as Mike attempts to take it from him. And then the gun goes off – BANG!

Symoné and Chrissy scream. The crowd scatters.

Mike falls on top of Craig Little. Craig Little pushes him off and gets up off the ground, with blood on his clothes and the 9mm still in his hand. He tucks the nine back into his pants.

"Fuck."

Mike is on the ground, balled up in a fetal position, holding his stomach; blood is all over his clothes and hands. Symoné breaks away from Willow and runs to help Mike. Chrissy is frozen in shock. Georgie and several of Mike's teammates come running out of the basketball court and find him on the ground, bleeding.

"Craig, why?" cries Symoné.

"Symoné, it happened so fast. I wasn't trying to shoot him. Mike grabbed the gun and it went off."

Sirens can be heard in a distance.

"Yo Little, we need to bounce," says Willow.

"Go Craig. I'm going to stay here with Mike until the ambulance comes," says Symoné.

Craig Little and Willow leave 155th Street.

Symoné kneels by Mike's body and cradles his head in her arm, while she applies pressure to his wound with her hand. She looks down at Mike with sadness and remorse. Tears are falling from her eyes. He looks up at her and tries to speak.

"Symoné, I . . ."

"Shh Mike, you need to save your strength."

"I . . . I love you."

"I know. I never stopped loving you. I was just . . ."

"I know . . . a . . . bout . . . My . . . kia."

"What?" Symoné is stunned.

"I didn't care . . . I love you, Symoné." Mike smiles, takes his last breath, and then closes his eyes.

Symoné is shaking Mike, trying to wake him up. "Mike, wake up!"

Chrissy, with tears falling down her face, walks over to Symoné and kneels beside her.

"He's gone, Symoné."

"He can't be, Chrissy, he can't be."

EMT arrives on the scene; Symoné and Chrissy sit back and allow them to work on Mike. They work vigorously to revive him, but are unsuccessful and stop.

"Why you stopped?"

"He's gone, miss."

"No, he's not."

Symoné shakes Mike's lifeless body and tries to wake him. "Wake up, you can't be dead! Baby please, wake up!"

Chrissy cries, as she watches Symoné trying to wake him.

"Miss please, you have to let him go now so we can do our job," says the police officer.

Chrissy's kneels down, gently touching Symoné's back. "We gotta let Mike go, Symoné."

Symoné looks at Chrissy. Chrissy takes Symoné's hand, helps her off the ground, and hugs her tight as Symoné cries hysterically in her arms.

❊ ❊ ❊

Eddie and Hershey are sitting on the sofa, counting stacks of money.

"Yo Hershey, how many more stacks you got to count over there? We got to get to the Rucker, Mike's playing in the championship."

"Yeah, I know. If you stop asking me every ten minutes how many more stacks I have to count, I'd be finished already."

Eddie glances down at the pager on his waist. "All these crazy numbers I don't know keep popping up on my beeper."

"Call them back."

"Nah, I don't call numbers I don't know."

There are several hard bangs on the door. Eddie and Hershey take their guns off the coffee table. Eddie walks over to the door and looks out of the peephole, and then tucks his 9mm into pant waist. He opens the door. Georgie is sweaty and out of breath.

"Georgie, why you knocking on my door like you five-o? And where's Mike?" Eddie sticks his head out the door and looks down the hallway.

"He's dead!"

"What?"

"They . . . they . . ."

"Georgie, calm down and catch your breath so I can understand you."

"They killed him."

"What you talking about, Georgie, killed who?" Eddie grabs Georgie up by his jersey and brings him into the house and closes the door. Georgie flops down on the sofa.

"Hershey, get him some water for me."

Hershey brings the water and gives it to Georgie.

"They killed Mike, Eddie."

"What?"

"Little shot Mike."

"Little shot Mike? Why, for what?" Eddie asks, and then sits on the sofa with a blank look on his face, and stares off into space.

"I don't know. They said it was an accident. At first they were talking, and then a fight broke out, and then shots."

"Eddie, what you wanna do, man?" asks Hershey.

Eddie does not respond.

"I got you, man. Just tell me when and how you wanna do it," says Hershey.

Eddie does not respond and continues to stare off into space.

❋   ❋   ❋

A couple of days after Mike's murder, Symoné is sitting at her dining room table in Ridgewood, New Jersey, finishing up a letter to her mother.

. . .I blame myself for the abuse you endured at the hands of Jack Fisher. I blame myself for Mike's death. He loved me unconditionally and I pushed him

away, because I was too ashamed to tell him, and you, about the rape and Jack being Mykia's father. I love Craig and need to tell him the truth if we are to have a happy, healthy future, even if it is from a prison cell. When I get back, I'll get some counseling and work out my issues. And, maybe we can get some counseling together. I would like us to work on building our mother and daughter relationship. I look forward to us spending more time together, just talking and raising Mykia. I love you, Mom.

Symoné

Symoné looks like she has not slept in days. Her eyes are red and puffy from crying. Her overnight bag is packed by the door, and Chrissy has Mykia fastened in her car seat.

Symoné hands the sealed envelope to Chrissy, who puts it in Mykia's baby bag.

"Could you give this letter to my mother when you drop Mykia off? Tell her it will explain everything."

"Symoné, I don't feel you going to D.C. to see Craig is a good idea right now."

"I talked to him and he needs me."

"Craig needs you? What about Mykia? She needs you. Did you forget Craig killed her father?"

"Chrissy, you don't understand, and I don't have the time to tell you now. I just need you to be a little more patient with me."

"I've been your best friend since first grade, through thick and thin, and now you don't have the time to talk to me?"

"No, you're taking it the wrong way, Chrissy."

"How am I supposed to take it?"

"Chrissy, have a seat. You're the first I'll tell the truth to."

"What is it, Symoné?"

"Mike is not Mykia's father."

"What?"

"I was raped by my father's partner, Jack."

"Oh my God, Symoné, I'm so sorry. Why didn't you tell me?"

"I tried to, but I was too ashamed."

"How have you dealt with this all by yourself?"

"It wasn't easy. Mike knew the whole time."

"How?"

"I don't know. I didn't know he knew. He told me the day he died. I blame myself for his death, and I can't hold onto this secret any longer. It has destroyed so many lives. This is why I need to talk to Craig."

"Just promise me you'll be careful. The police want him, and Eddie's on the warpath."

"I'll be okay."

Chrissy puts her arms around Symoné and comforts her with a long hug, then picks up the car seat that holds Mykia. Symoné grabs her overnight bag and they leave.

❊ ❊ ❊

Chrissy rings the doorbell to Mae's house. Mae opens the door. Some of her bruises are still visible from the beating she endured at the hands of Jack Fisher. She's surprised to see Chrissy.

"Hello Mrs. Harris."

"Hello Chrissy. Where's Symoné?"

Chrissy comes into the house, and they sit on the sofa.

"She had a plane to catch to D.C."

"D.C.?"

"Yes, she went to see Craig and said she will call you once she gets settled."

"Craig? What is she thinking? Aren't the police looking for him?"

"I think she wants to try to get Craig to give himself up."

"I wish she would have talked to me first."

"It's been a rough week, Mrs. Harris. I need get back home and start packing for school."

"That's right it's the end of August. I sure wish you put some sense into Symoné head and get her to join you at Spelman."

"I'll try."

"Well, have a safe trip back."

"Thanks." Chrissy gives Mae a hug and leaves

"Now Nana got Mykia all to herself." Mae smothers Mykia with hugs and kisses, then takes off her clothes and goes through her baby bag, searching for her nightclothes. She finds Symoné's letter, opens it, and reads.

Dear Mom,

I want to start this letter off by saying thank you for all you have done for Mykia and me. I know at times I have been very difficult and not easy to get along with. I apologize for that and promise to be a better daughter.

I wrote this letter, because so many things have happened in these last weeks and it got me thinking. All these bad things that happened to you, Mike, and Craig could have been avoided if I had you sooner about Jack and the rape.

Jack was an evil man and I am glad that he's dead and do not regret killing him. My only regret is that I did not do it long ago before he had the chance to hurt you . . .

Mae stops reading, picks Mykia up, holds her closes to her chest, and breaks down.

❋ ❋ ❋

It's 5 p.m. The clouds hang low and heavy in the sky. A storm is coming. Craig Little pulls up and parks his 4Runner in front of his townhouse, at the Brummel Court in Northwest, D.C. He gets out and has a small Tiffany & Co box in his hands. He puts the box into his jacket pocket and grabs the groceries out the back. There are a couple of cars parked in the courtyard spaces.

A Jeep Wrangler is parked a few feet away from Craig Little's townhouse. A bald-headed, very dark-skin man, with a Washington Wizards flat-brimmed hat and jersey, is fixing a flat tire on the Wrangler. He notices the man working on the car, and then opens the door and goes into the house. Symoné meets Craig Little at the door with a kiss and takes one of the bags from him into the kitchen. He puts the other bags down on the floor by the door and peeks out the window. The man and the Jeep Wrangler are gone.

"Symoné, have you noticed any strange guys hanging around the house lately?"

"No. Why?"

"Nothing; never mind."

Craig Little sneaks up behind Symoné in the kitchen, gives her a hug and kiss, and then pulls out the small box, putting it on the counter in front of Symoné. She picks up the box and turns around to open it. It's an 18-carat white gold band, with a round cut, 4-carat diamond engagement ring. She is speechless.

"Well, aren't you going to say something, jump up and down, call your mother, call Chrissy?"

"I don't know what to say."

"Yes, you'll marry me?"

"Of course, but we need to talk," she says, and then closes the box and puts it back on the counter.

Craig Little picks the box up. "You love me?"

"Of course I do."

Craig Little puts the engagement ring on Symoné's finger, and then his pager goes off.

"I got to pick up this money. When I get back we'll go to the Chart House Restaurant and celebrate." Craig Little kisses Symoné and heads back out the door.

The courtyard parking spaces have filled up with people home from work. The man and the Wrangler are back. Craig Little opens the door and he sees the man fiddling on the inside hood with two men in overalls. He walks over to get into his 4Runner.

"Excuse me, buddy, you got a jumper cable we can use?" asks one of the men in overalls.

Craig Little is hesitant. "Yeah, I have it in the house, give me a minute." He turns and walks back to the front door of his townhouse, puts the key in the door, and turns around. The man in overalls is directly behind him, pushing Craig Little against the door. Craig Little realizes it's a hit.

The hit man quickly unzips his overalls, pulls out a Desert Eagle Semi-Automatic, and aims. Without fear Craig Little looks the hit man in the eyes, turns his shoulders so he is diagonal to the hit man, and grabs hold of the gun's barrel. A bullet tears a big hole through the side of the front door. He stuns the hit man with a hard right across face, and the hit man stumbles back. Craig Little quickly pushes open the front door, closes and locks it behind him.

"Symoné," he calls out, "Symoné!"

Symoné comes running out of the kitchen with a bottle of cherry soda in her hand. She sees Craig Little tearing up the living room, tossing the sofa cushions toward the floor.

"What's going on?"

"I need you to get upstairs, now."

Craig Little pulls a Tech 9 and a Mac 11 from the sofa.

BANG!

Symoné is startled by the loud noise and drops her soda bottle on the floor.

"Go Symoné, now!"

Craig Little pushes Symoné toward the stairs. She rushes up. He raises the Tec 9 in one hand and the Mac 11 in the other and shoots.

Huge holes are beginning to form through the front door from the powerful gun blasts. Hershey, Eddie's enforcer, is in the Wizard Jersey and hat, standing in the doorway with a sawed-off shotgun. He throws the shotgun down and pulls two 9mms from under his jersey, aims at Craig Little and shoots. After pumping several shots into Little's body, Hershey stops and the three hit men walk into the house through the massive hole in the door. Then Hershey picks up where he left off, while the first hit man aims and shoots his Desert Eagle, and the second shoots his Street Sweeper.

The power of the weapons tear through Craig Little's flesh. Large amounts of blood splatter the wall red.

❋ ❋ ❋

Symoné peaks out the upstairs bedroom and sees Craig Little and his guns in a pool of blood at the bottom of the stairs. She is terrified and shuts the door, then runs over to the dresser and pushes it across the floor. Then she picks up the telephone and dials 911.

❋ ❋ ❋

"You heard that?" Hershey says.

"Nah, I didn't hear anything," First Hit Man says.

"Me neither," Second Hit Man says.

"Shh, be quiet. One of ya'll go outside and watch the door," Hershey commands.

Hershey aims his 9mms and carefully heads up the stairs toward the bedroom, with a hit man behind him.

❋ ❋ ❋

Symoné is whispering into the telephone.

"Hello?"

"Hello 911 Operator. Caller, where's the emergency?"

"Brummel Court."

"I can't hear you, caller. Could you please repeat that?"

"Brummel . . ." Symoné hears the men at the door and then several shots are fired.

"Hello . . . Hello . . . Caller?"

Symoné drops the telephone, runs over to the window, opens it, looks down, hesitates, and then jumps two stories onto the green lawn below. She is hurt, but manages to get up and limps toward the courtyard.

Hershey and the hit man force the door open, find the bedroom empty, and the window wide open. Hershey notices the telephone on the floor near the window, the receiver off the hook. He and the hit man run over to the window and look out and see Symoné limping to the courtyard. Hershey shoots at Symoné, the bullets barely missing her. The hit man jumps out the window. He yelps out in pain when he lands, hurting his ankle. But he gets up, steadily aiming his automatic, and shoots. Symoné is hit with a riddle of bullets in the back and falls to the ground.

Police sirens are growing loud in the distance. Neighbors open their doors and come out into the streets, walking toward Symoné.

Hershey and the hit man rush toward the Wrangler and speed away in the opposite direction of the gathering crowd.

Symoné lies on the ground in a pool of her own blood. She holds tight to the locket around her neck, tears fall from her eyes; and then she takes her last breath.

❊   ❊   ❊

Many years later Symone's daughter Mykia is graduating from her grandfather's Alma mater, John Jay College, with a Master's in Criminal Justice.

Mae sits in the crowd at the commencement ceremony with her head high as she watches her grandchild, the Valedictorian of her class, give her speech.

"...But, we know that it is you, our family and friends, who made us what we are to today and gave us the tools we needed to achieve this accomplishment.

My grandma, Mae, a retired nurse, who raised me and sacrificed most her life caring for others. She is a model of strength and a living example of the power of faith. My boyfriend Darius Blue, sorry for all of the romantic dates I had to cancel so I could study..."

The audience roars with laughter.

"You know those times when I was like, 'I can't talk, my legal research and writing brief is due tomorrow.' I want to say thank you for being there throughout all the madness and for your support.

And lastly, my mother, Symoné Harris, who passed when I was just a toddler; life is like a box of chocolates, and you never know what you're gonna get. Life is a mystery that we come to comprehend as we bite into each new day and no one knows what will happen tomorrow – the outcome is unexpected and unpredictable. I realized that it was not always the obstacle I had been faced with that defined me, but rather how I overcame it and what I became from it as a result.

I hope you all live up to your greatest potential as lawyers, policy makers, and entrepreneurs. It's been an honor taking this journey with you, Class of 2020.

For now, savor the goodbyes and welcome the new beginnings."

The audience rises as one in a standing ovation for Mykia Lorendale Harris. Then the graduates turn their tassels and throw their miter board caps in the air.

CHILD SEXUAL ABUSE DOES NOT DISCRIMINATE. IT'S NOT A MATTER OF CLASS OR PREFERENCE, RACE OR RELIGION, MALE OR FEMALE, AND THE PERPETRATORS COME IN MANY DISGUISES.

> **"CHILDREN TRULY HAVE NO SAFE HAVEN FROM VICTIMIZATIONS, BECAUSE THEY ARE VULNERABLE BOTH WITHIN AND OUTSIDE THEIR HOMES; IN THE COMPANY OF THOSE THEY KNOW LIES THE POTENTIAL FOR ABUSE."**
>
> **- DEBORAH R. MOODY**

READING GROUP GUIDE

A Letter to Readers

A Penny for Your Thoughts

Excerpt from Lorendale's Law: Fallen Petals Aftermath

Dear Readers,

Many of you have asked if "Fallen Petals" is my story. I was not conceived by rape, but a victim of child sexual abuse. I was only ten years old.

Declaration of a new doctor

Now, as a new doctor, I solemnly promise that I will, to the best of my ability, serve humanity – caring for the sick, promoting good health, and alleviating pain and suffering.

I recognize that the practice of medicine is a privilege with which comes considerable responsibility and I will not abuse my position.

I shall never intentionally do or administer anything to the overall harm of my patients.

My child molester was a pediatric podiatrist. Years, after the incident I went to counseling and even confronted my molester, hoping to get some explanation and reasoning behind his actions, but there was none.

With all that knowledge about child abuse today, the child molester and the effects on the victim, it is still a topic that is considered taboo in our society. A topic victims rather hide due to fear of being shunned or embarrassed.

I am out of the closet, exposing my fears, and myself hoping that my story helps others. Abuse is not normal, but your feelings and emotions afterward are. Do we forget or get over it, no. We learn to cope. Coping, surrounding yourself with people that love you unconditionally and people you feel comfortable talking to are key.

I waited too long before I started to share my story with family and friends. How many more children have been victimized by this doctor, because of my silence?

I would like to ask that if any of my readers have been a victim or know someone in this situation, stop what you are doing and pick up a phone. The longer you wait, the more people will be victimized.

Yours sincerely,
Tiffany Simoné

A PENNY FOR YOUR THOUGHTS

1. Do you think Detective Jack Fisher regrets murdering his partner and best friend Detective Vaughn Harris?

2. After Vaughn's death, do you think both age and loneliness played a major factor in Mae dating his partner and subjecting herself to domestic violence?

3. Who do you think Symoné loved more, Mike Blackwell or Craig Little, and why?

4. Do you think Symoné is to blame for everyone's demise, and if not who is and why?

5. Do you think Symoné's reaction after the rape was typical and realistic of a victim in her situation, and why?

THE FOLLOWING IS A SAMPLE CHAPTER FROM

TIFFANY SIMONÉ'S

EAGERLY ANTICIPATED SEQUEL TO

FALLEN PETALS: THE DECEPTION, THE DECEIT, & THE DAMNED

LORENDALE'S LAW: FALLEN PETALS AFTERMATH

VISIT AUTHOR'S WEBSITE FOR RELEASE DATE ON THIS SUSPENSE THRILLER

TIFFANYSIMONETHEWRITER.COM

TO NEW BEGINNINGS

. . . .

CHAPTER 1

The psychotherapist Dr. Ginger Grey's private practice is located on the top floor in a luxury high-rise on Sutton Place and 56th Street in New York City. When you walk through the doors, the soothing sounds of the ocean and relaxing classical music can be heard coming from the built-in wall speakers. Dr. Grey waits in front of the elevator bank, with her card key in a slot on the wall that opens the outer brass elevator doors, allowing her clients access up to her office.

The door opens and Mykia Lorendale Harris steps out. She is a tall, well-dressed, stunningly beautiful, needs very little make up, with a flawless coco complexion, and her dark brown silky hair long, with a part on the side and swiped partially across her forehead. She is in need of counseling to help her cope with a dark family secret she recently found out about.

"Hello Miss Harris," Dr. Grey says and extends her hand.

"Hello Dr. Grey," she says with downcast eyes and shakes the doctor's hand.

"I'm glad you were finally able to make it. Have a seat in the waiting area, help yourself to the refreshments in the corner, and I'll be with you shortly."

"Okay," Mykia says and then studies Dr. Grey as she walks into her office. Mykia is amazed to see that the mature, distinctive voice she spoke to a few times over the phone was a fresh-faced, attractive white woman with an athletic build. She has short red hair, piercing blue eyes, and freckles. She also has style. Her outfit is vintage right down to her cat-shaped eyeglasses. Mykia thinks, *I hope she's as good as she looks.*

Mykia takes a seat on the paisley-printed loveseat. She notices the living room has been turned into a cozy waiting area decorated in muted earth tones. The vertical blinds are partially open, allowing some sunlight in. There are several *Psychology Today* magazines on the cherry wood end table. Expensive pictures and prints adorn the walls. There is a large fish tank built in the wall with different types of exotic fish. An antique coffee table is set up in the corner with a Keurig Platinum Coffee Brewing System. She exhales, a slight smile forms across her face, and she nods her head in approval

The door to Dr. Grey's office opens. "Come on in, Miss Harris. I'm ready to see you now," she says in a calm, pleasant tone.

They enter the office and Dr. Grey closes the door behind them, sealing out the music from the waiting area. "Please have a seat wherever you are most comfortable, the chair or sofa." She sits in her swivel high-back leather chair and waits for Mykia to settle in.

Mykia relaxes in the Chester Aniline Leather chair and puts her legs across the matching ottoman.

"What brings you to my office today?"

Mykia sits back and exhales deeply. "Well . . ." She hesitates, then swallows and clears her throat, before she starts to speak again.

Dr. Grey listens carefully.

"I was just a toddler when my mom died. I was always an inquisitive child. The older I got the more inquisitive I became about my life. I often wondered about the circumstances behind my mother's death, as well as what she was like growing up — how she wore her hair, what she smelled like, etc. And every time I would ask my grandma about my mother it saddened her. Her eyes watered and I could tell it was painful to talk about it. She would put me on her lap, hold me close, look in my eyes, and say, 'The Lord felt it fit to take your mama because he needed her more in heaven.' I would turn up my face and think it wasn't fair, but who was I to question God." Mykia shrugs her shoulders. "My father on the other hand was a mystery. I didn't know if he was dead or alive and the mention of him made my grandma uneasy. The look on her face frightened me the first time I asked her about my father. She gave me this unblinking death stare, like she was a lion about to attack. For a few seconds she didn't move or speak. It was like she was in a trance and then abruptly said, 'I don't want to talk about him.' And that was the end of the conversation, and the last time I asked."

Mykia shifted in her chair to get into a more comfortable position. She rests her head back, closes her eyes smiles, and then continues to speak. "For a long time it was just me and my grandma against the world." Her voice starts to crack. She pauses for a moment. "We did everything together – cook, shop, dinner outings, concerts, Broadway shows, and vacation twice a year. There were times I found her to be a bit overprotective." She smiles, drops her head, and continues, "I remember when she brought me my first cell phone. She made me put my hand on the Bible and swear that when I stayed out late at night with friends that I would keep her posted on my whereabouts, and I did just that. She spoiled me. I didn't want for nothing and I had the best education money could buy. I could tell her everything and kept no secrets from her. She was my best friend." Mykia pauses again and stares off into the distance. Tears start welling in her eyes.

Dr. Grey hands Mykia a box of Kleenex. "Are you okay?"

Mykia nods her head yes and wipe her eyes with a tissue.

"We can stop here and pick things up in another session, if you'd like:

"No. I need to get this out," and Mykia continues telling her story. "For an elderly woman, Grandma Mae was relatively healthy, except for the occasional ache and pain, which was normal for a woman in her seventies. She received her annual flu vaccine, like she did every year. They developed a vaccine designed for people 65 and older, but she had an allergic reaction to the vaccine . . . and . . . died soon after." Silent tears roll down her face and her nose is running. She pulls a tissue from the box, wipes her tears, and blows her nose.

"I cried for days. I felt empty and lost after my grandma's death. Then the time came when I needed to go through her belongings, pack everything up, and donate to Goodwill. The thought of this task made me ill and sent chills through my body. At the time I didn't know why I felt this way, but I would soon find out," she says, as the muscles in her face tighten and her voice sounds empty.

Dr. Grey notices Mykia's sudden mood change. She discreetly drops her eyeglasses onto the lower bridge of her nose and peers over them. She tilts her head to one side while listening.

"My boyfriend Darius – he's the best," she says, then sits up, adjusts herself slightly in the chair, and a brief smile appears on her face.

Dr. Grey can tell by Mykia's body language and facial expression how much she loves Darius.

"Darius came with me to my grandma's house. Together we packed each room, one by one. I cleaned out the draws of her nightstand and I found a letter. It was addressed to my grandma from my mother. I hid the letter from Darius because I wanted to read it by myself." She inhales deeply and sighs. "The truth was there. My entire lift unfolded in one letter . . . who I really was . . . an accident, the product of a monster who raped my mother."

Mykia lowers her head and the room falls silent.

❋   ❋   ❋

Weeks have gone by since Mykia's grandmother died and her visit to Dr. Grey's office. She wants badly to forget the painful truth of her past and wishes she had never found or read the letter. She thinks, *why didn't I just throw the letter away? It wasn't addressed to me. It wasn't mine to read.*

She blames her curiosity for her misery, but then tries to shift the blame on her grandma for not throwing the letter away a long time ago. She thinks to herself, *why did Grandma keep the letter? Did she want someone to find it? Why didn't she just leave the past in the past?*

Mykia is angry, hurt, and confused. She is looking for someone to blame for her torment because she is unable to cope with her feelings and thoughts. She starts isolating herself and avoiding physical and emotional contact with others, including Darius. She buries herself in her work, preparing case briefs for other lawyers at the Manhattan District Attorney's Office. As much as she tries to avoid the inevitable, when she sees her reflection in the mirror, it is a constant reminder of the past. She often thinks to herself, *I have no real family. I'm a bastard child who was conceived by rape.*

When Mykia is home alone at night, she turns off all the phones so she can get some peace and quiet from the outside world and Darius's round-the-clock interrogation about what's wrong with her. Once in bed it's hard for her to sleep with so much on her mind. She often finds herself removing her mother's letter from the nightstand, reading them over and over, analyzing its contents. She usually cries herself to sleep.

❋ ❋ ❋

Dr. Ginger Grey is holding her monthly support group for individuals conceived by rape in a lounge at Silent Voices United Adult Center in Harlem. The lounge is warm and inviting. Several people are sitting on a black u-shaped couch with animal-print throw pillows. There are a few people at the buffet table in the corner.

Dr. Grey stands by a folding chair at the opening of the couch, sipping tea and chatting with Mykia.

"It's been a while," says Dr. Grey.

"After our first session I thought I could handle it on my own, but I was wrong. I decided to try the support group, maybe it could help me through this difficult time," Mykia replies.

"It is important to share your experience to help you get through the anger, depression, and other emotions that you may be going through." Ginger gently touches Mykia's shoulder. "It is normal to be nervous, but it is important that you also take that first step to acknowledge the circumstances that brought you here today."

"Every day I look in the mirror I acknowledge it – the horrible truth. I just want it to go away."

"Horrible? Life is beautiful." Dr. Grey is silent for a moment and appears to reminisce, and then a slight smile comes across her face. "Life is what we make it, and regardless of how we got here we have the right to life, to make a difference and change the minds of those that believe otherwise."

"Thank you, Dr. Grey. I needed to hear that," Mykia says.

"Call me Ginger. It's not formal in the support group."

"Okay, Ginger," she says with a slight smile and then looks down at her vibrating iPhone. It's a text from Darius.

I hope u not working 2 hard. Don't forget we have dinner reservations tonight at 8.

"Put my number into your phone and if you ever need to talk at any time, day or night, do not hesitate."

Mykia enters Ginger's number into her iPhone, takes a seat on the couch, and texts Darius back.

I'll see u at 8. Love u.

Ginger looks at her watch. It reads seven o'clock. "Hello everyone. At this time I would like to ask everyone to take a seat so we can get started."